Dealing

or

The Berkeley-to-Boston Forty-Brick Lost-Bag Blues

Dealing

OR

The Berkeley-to-Boston Forty-Brick Lost-Bag Blues

a novel by

"MICHAEL DOUGLAS"

Alfred A. Knopf/New York/1971

THIS IS A BORZOI BOOK
PUBLISHED BY ALFRED A. KNOPF, INC.

 Published in the United States
by Alfred A. Knopf, Inc., New York, and simultaneously in
Canada by Random House of Canada, Toronto.
Distributed by Random House, Inc., New York.
Library of Congress Catalog Card Number: 70–127093
Portions of this book first appeared in *Playboy* Magazine.
Manufactured in the United States of America

FIRST EDITION

ALL NAMES, CHARACTERS, AND EVENTS IN THIS BOOK ARE FICTIONAL, AND ANY RE-SEMBLANCE TO REAL PERSONS IS EITHER COINCIDENTAL OR THE RESULT OF STONED PARANOIA.

To the lawmakers of our great land:

Play This Book LOUD!

Most of what my neighbors call good,
I am profoundly convinced is
evil, and if I repent anything, it is
my good conduct that I repent.

THOREAU

When somebody like Timothy Leary
comes out and justifies [using
drugs], we've got to jump on him
with hobnailed boots.

LINKLETTER

I knew I was going off (hard)
drugs when I didn't like to watch TV.

BILLIE HOLLIDAY

Contents

1
Viper's Tangle

The sky is high, and so am I—
if you'se a viper.

FATS WALLER

1

As a standby you get the seat right behind the jets. Sit down, tuck the special suitcase under the seat in front of you, buckle up, and look out the window at the Boston rain. Then look over and smile at the two Marines sitting next to you, and wait for the goddamned thing to take off.

Once in the air, you get your choice of chicken, swordfish, or roast beef; *Life, Vogue,* or *Sports Afield. Life* features an article on the growing menace to our children, the Marijuana Habit. A follow-up on how one Illinois town rallied to the challenge and pulled itself out of the dope gutter. A quote from a kid at the University of Illinois who says reality is the best trip of all.

When you can't stand any more, you up and amble back to the can and flip on the OCCUPIED sign. Once safely locked in, you fumble around with the air whooshing up out of the john; you try not to spill your whole stash on the floor as you roll a neat little joint in your clammy dope-fiend hands. And then you blow it.

After that, things slow down a bit and you amble back and stumble across the two Marines and get your earphones on just in time to catch the flick. Last time it wasn't too bad, some Nazis torturing a prostitute, but no such luck on these daytime ventures—it's Andy Griffith as an iconoclastic but truly lovable parish priest. For the next two hours you are part of Andy's G-for-

General-Audiences struggle to refurnish the church, and it's all pretty wonderful. But toward the end of the movie, high-altitude dehydration sets in, and you find yourself feeling pretty miserable. So you amble back toward the can again, with numerous eyes flicking up at you suspiciously as you walk down the aisle—since everybody smelled dope the *last* time—but you fool them all and get a cup of water.

While you're in the galley you pocket a few of those absurd little booze bottles that they hustle for a buck apiece before the meal, have a few more cups of water, turning occasionally to face the cabin, and smile innocently at anyone who is looking. Then return to your seat, with some ice in the cup, to get thoroughly and quietly juiced.

This doesn't help the dehydration any but it makes the time go a lot faster. Toward the end of the trip you even join the Marines in molesting the stewardesses. The stewardesses are very good-natured about them, because they're in uniform, poor fellows, and so young, too. The stewardesses are less good-natured about you.

Finally the captain comes on to announce that San Francisco airport is still there, and that we may be landing soon. The seat belt sign comes on, the Muzak returns, and everyone frantically puffs away, trying to get that last little hit of nicotine before the NO SMOKING sign flashes on. Behind you in the next seat the middle-aged lady searches her purse for the tranquilizer she always drops before the landing.

And then the plane comes down. It's 3:55 P.M. Pacific Standard Time, seventy-two degrees, the sun is shining on both sides of the street, and it's all before you.

2

I was expecting to be met at the airport, but nobody showed. I couldn't believe John hadn't called my friends to let them know I was coming, so I shuffled up and down the arrivals platform waiting for a familiar face. Everyone was waiting. There were servicemen waiting for the bus, businessmen waiting for the fat wife and the dog, porters waiting for tips; all of us waiting to see what would happen and waiting then to see what would come next.

After an hour I knew John hadn't called. It pissed me off that he could be so casual. He could afford to be, that was the heart of the matter. John had enough bread to buy himself out of anything that he got into—and into anything he felt out of. He simply assumed things were the same for other people—and if they didn't measure up to the assumption, then what the hell were they doing hanging around with him? But I was still angry, because I couldn't take a bus across the Bay, not with twenty-five hundred in twenties bulging in my coat pocket. The only alternative was a rented car, and he knew that I didn't have the bread to waste on a rented car. But then, he did . . .

So I went over to the Hertz counter, where a sleazy blonde in a zebra suit was smiling into space. She could be easily replaced by a machine that smiled, I thought as I stepped into view. But then a machine would have known that my license was a phony. And anyway it was all part of the game: I gave her the license and she smiled. I pretended the smile was real, and she pretended the license was real. A reasonable bargain, all things considered.

The car was a green '69 Mustang. First thing I did when I got in was to check the ashtray. A ridiculous gesture, but the kind of thing I always find myself doing, just to make sure that the ads are really up front. Yeah. Well, the ashtray was clean but the ignition was burned out and the car wouldn't start, so I exchanged it for an identical green Mustang and rolled out to Berkeley.

Back on the Bay Shore Freeway. It felt good to be ripping along at sixty-five miles an hour, a cool salty breeze blowing in off the water and the blue-green hills of the city up ahead. It was almost five, and the outbound lanes were mobbed, sweaty tangles of bumper-to-bumper frustration. But there was barely another car on my side of the road. I suddenly thought of Boston, and I laughed. It would be raining there, still, and the streets would be filled with the long, dour faces of people trying to convince themselves that spring really was on its way—or at least would be once exams were over. Boston seemed so far away, and so ridiculous. Just then I rounded a corner and the whole side of a hill bade me WELCOME TO SAN FRANCISCO.

I realized that I shouldn't let myself get too carried away, that I should stay cool for the work ahead. But I felt so good about being back in California that I just couldn't feel anything else. I couldn't get uptight about meeting Musty, and I couldn't feel all the small, sobering, paranoiac things that I should've been feeling, that I was supposed to be feeling. Just before I'd left Boston, John had given me the rundown on Musty, so that I could get good and paranoid about doing business with him. Being paranoid was supposed to make me cautious, discreet, cool about the whole riff. But what John told me just made me more confident than ever.

Because Musty was big. At twenty-three he was one of the biggest and most successful dealers in the country.

Which meant that his scene was a lot different from most other dealers'. Most of them, when they're doing lots of ten or fifteen or twenty bricks at a time, think they're moving a lot of dope. They figure they've got a good hustle going, and for the most part, they do. But they've got one hang-up, and that is their dependence on a supplier. In that respect they're as helpless as the little guy who picks up a street lid now and then on his way home from work. And they can get burned and ripped off and hustled in a thousand different ways, just like that little guy.

Because they're not in control of what's going down. They're just taking part.

Musty was in control. He did only one kind of job, and he did it extraordinarily well. Musty ran lots of two thousand kilos—no more, no less on any given run —across the border from Mexico. He dumped them in San Diego, in his own warehouses, and there they sat until they were shipped out in broken-down lots to New York. Musty kept his hand in the operation up to the point when the bricks were shipped, his own art-supplies front doing the job. But after that he was through with it; he took his cut and split. That way anything that was busted, either in New York, or on the way back to California, was almost impossible to pin on him. For all the narcs ever knew, the stuff was coming in through the New York Port Authority, right under their noses.

Musty ran a tight operation, with everyone from the Federales to the Customs people to the Mexicans who drove the trucks and airplanes being liberally paid off. He wasn't just careful, though; he had class. When it came time for a shipment, he went down to the Mexican plantations himself. He was friends with the plantation owners he bought from and he spoke fluent Spanish. His concern did not go unnoticed by the sellers, and as a result his marijuana was only the purest, his bricks the heaviest. They were almost always at least thirty-two ounces—dry—with very few sticks and no stones or clay. On a market that's usually full of oregano and gasoline-cured or otherwise hopelessly souped-up garbage, his dope was highly regarded. And it always brought a good price.

The most impressive thing about his operation was that he'd been running it for almost four years without a hint of trouble or a cramp in his style. A record like that demands respect, whether you're behind the law or trying to keep ahead of it. The IRS people in San Diego had finally gotten on his back a few months before, but it'd been nothing serious, just a lot of irritating questions, and he'd simply stepped out of town for a while. To San Francisco, which was now his company headquarters.

3

John had met Musty earlier in the spring, on the Massachusetts Turnpike. John was test-driving the Ferrari he'd gotten the week before, seeing how it performed on the road. And Musty was bumming around the East, California style, with a pack on his back and his thumb out dangling. So John had picked him up and they were rolling along at maybe eighty, nobody saying anything and Musty no doubt sitting there thinking, What a bummer this is, to ride in this car with a straight creep —thinking this because in California anybody who smokes dope looks like he smokes dope, and Musty wasn't used to the Eastern style yet. So when John, with his maroon Ferrari and his J. Press suit and his Newport accent, opened the glove compartment to reveal a pound bag of clean Michoácan, Musty blew his mind. The dope had come from one of Musty's kilos that was nothing but buds and flowers to begin with; he just started laughing, while he rolled a few joints. John rolled up the windows so the smoke wouldn't get out, and they both managed to get high as the sky before they hit the Newton tolls.

Which is a sad pun, for hit the Newton toll booth they did, going about twenty-five. Drove right up the cement fender and piled into the little box the toll guy stands in. Seemed that John, who was never a good driver, had a little trouble maneuvering his machine after a few joints. The toll guy was terrified, expecting to find some epileptic old lady who'd had a coronary. Instead, he was greeted by two very stoned young men, laughing hysterically and wiping the tears from their eyes. Completely unscathed, both of them, but not looking particularly grateful for it.

When the cop came, he told John that he was a very lucky guy. The cop also said some other things about Rich Motherfuckers and Kids Today. Everybody is interested in Kids Today, even the cops. He asked John how he happened to total his brand new Ferrari and John explained about the faulty disc brakes—these crummy little Italian imports, you know, they're all the same—and the cop farted.

Then he drove John and Musty back to a gas station where they could call for someone to pick them up. John sat in the front seat, because he had a suit on and looked respectable. Musty sat in the back. The cop talked to John first, giving him some more about Rich Motherfuckers and Damage to Public Property and asking how his old man liked picking up the tab. Then the cop looked in the rear-view mirror and asked Musty how long it had been since he had taken a bath and whether he thought he was Jesus Christ, with hair like that. The cop also said he had fought in the war, he wanted them both to know, in the goddamn war.

To change the subject, John suggested that it must be tough work to be a state trooper. The cop mellowed at this and admitted that it was tough work. Everybody thought it was a great job to be a state trooper, he said. Everybody thought it was all glory and gravy. Everybody wanted to be a trooper, but they didn't have no fucking idea, it was hard work and no joke.

John got off with a State Warning. Musty was told to be out of the state within forty-eight hours.

That was the way John worked. He needed to be with a person only about fifteen minutes before he knew what his weak spot was, and how to go to work on him. It didn't matter if that person was a cop, or a professor, or a freak. Fifteen minutes. Anyway, John'd put his finger on Musty's weak spot as efficiently as he'd managed the trooper. And before Musty said goodbye to Massachusetts, he'd agreed to sell dope to John in small lots, so long as the pickup was made on the West Coast. Musty, who never did anything less than two thousand kilos, and never touched his dope after it was in San Diego.

So I was on my way to meet Musty.

4

Traffic was heavier going over the Bay Bridge, but I made the corner of Ashby and Telegraph by five-thirty. From there it was just a few blocks to Musty's address, 339 Holly Street, in the middle of a quiet neighborhood of clean, pink-and-white stuccos with palm trees and clipped lawns. There was nobody on the street to stare at the straight honky who jumped out of a green Mustang with a suitcase in his hand and went up to ring 339.

The suitcase was a little thing John had rigged up, small enough to fit under an airplane seat, and lined with aluminum to keep the dope smell in. It also had internal and external locks to disappoint inquisitive cops. A sealed package of any sort requires a specific search warrant before it can be legally opened. Altogether a neat and reassuring way to travel.

I rang the buzzer beneath the name on the mailbox: Padraic O'Shaugnessy. No wonder they called him Musty. Then I waited, and when nothing happened I pushed the buzzer again. The apartment was on the second floor, and I could faintly hear it ringing up there. But nothing else, no footsteps or talking or other noise.

I began to get irritated, because I was right on time and they should have been there to open the door for me when I came up the steps. I couldn't figure out where they could be, but then I didn't really give a damn. I just didn't dig standing around like the Fuller Brush man, waiting for somebody to come to the door.

Finally I went back to the car and started reading the *Tribe* I'd picked up on Telegraph. What a drag it was, this waiting. I pulled out my own little traveling stash, rolled a joint, and blew it, trying to relax.

I'd been sitting there half an hour when I decided to get something to eat. I could never eat on planes, and after the six-hour flight I was hungry as hell. The stoned hungries, I might add, which is what the Now Generation is all about. A normal case of the hungries anyone with a will can sit out, but the stoned hungries are merciless. When dope eventually gets legalized, it'll be the A & P lobby that's responsible. How can you argue against a drug that keeps you eating regularly, sleeping regularly, and buying a six-pack of Pepsi every day? No way, in America.

I'd just started the car when I heard sirens. I was wondering how close the fire was, when the patrol cars came screeching around the corner, going the wrong way on a one-way street, and pulled up in front of 339. Behind the patrol cars were two Ford sedans, loaded with narcs. They had a cop driving, so it looked like they weren't just dropping in to pass the time of day. I sank down in my seat, and waited.

The bust moved very quickly, and very efficiently. The cops jumped out of the patrol cars and staked the house out, three in the rear and three up front. Two others headed for the front door; one had an ax and one had a portable vacuum cleaner.

The narcs spread out behind the cops, five of them going into the house. They were fingering their lapels and hitching up their pants nervously, like they expected some trouble. Which was absurd, because anyone as big as Musty wouldn't hassle cops. But it appeared from my bucket-seat foxhole as though they might be planning to shoot first and ask questions later. Oakland heat, it will be remembered, have that habit.

I was afraid to leave. I suddenly realized why John had been so insistent on my looking straight, and so insistent on my schedule. It looked like the man had finally come down on Musty. If I took off, one of the plainclothesmen standing near me might notice the car and take down the plate numbers. And then, if he decided to check and found out that the car had been rented that afternoon at the airport by a kid from Cambridge, Massachusetts, well, that'd be Fat City for the narcs.

So I stayed. And I sweated it, because the bust was shooting one of our little rules to hell. The Three Day Rule. It was nothing more than a rule of thumb that we always worked by: the heat were usually at least three days behind anything that was happening. More likely five days, to be sure, but for safety we usually kept our schedule down to three. So the courier always flew in within three days of Musty's run from S.D., and got out of town within three days of the pickup. It was cool to work that way, because the heat simply couldn't move any faster than that. I mean, the heat are only people. They've got a job, and for eight hours a day they do it. But after that they go home and watch the box with the wife and kids, like everybody else. And so if you worked full time, the way we did, it was easy to stay ahead of them.

But here they were, and here I was, curled up in fetal position on the seat, peeping over the dashboard at the plainclothes narc nearest me. He was watching the house. He didn't look too interested. In fact, he looked bored shitless. The cops-and-robbers glow began to fade close up, and as the bust progressed I got more and more into this dude. He had his hands in his pockets now, and was staring at the street. God, what a drag, I suddenly thought. What an unbelievable bitch of a drag it must be to work as a narc, and spend your whole life rushing around town trying to bust a few druggies. It was a unique train of thought for me to take, because narcs have achieved a certain hard-earned prominence in the mythology of dope smoking. They're cast as relentless, evil, and thoroughly mindless cogs in the great machine of repression. Wowie zowie. This guy didn't look evil, he didn't look like much of anything. Just a tired, dull, underpaid stool for the law.

But then I thought, What the hell. I wasn't going to get suckered into that routine again, into thinking of that pig as just another person. Because he wasn't, and it was dangerous to think of him as if he were. The danger was a personal one. I'd just be setting myself up for a rip-off if I ever got into any kind of hassle with the dude.

Because if I got into a hassle, I'd still be a person, but he'd have to be a pig. It'd happened to me so many times, that whole riff. Like you talk to any cop who's hassling, and after a while—if you come on like a regular chum—after a while, he'll swear up and down that he's Real Sorry To Have To Do This To You. He'll tell you that if it weren't for the blue he's wearing, he'd take you home to have a beer and meet the wife. But then he'll lay it on you: he's real sorry, and you're supposed to understand because you're a regular chum, but he's got no choice but to run you in. His job is to enforce the law. And then it'll all come tumbling out, all the excuses, all the lies, all the jive about how he doesn't have anything to do with anything. He's just doing his job, and he's not really running you in. It's the law, and he can't change the law, he just has to do his job, so . . . so? On go the cuffs, and on go the masks—and off you go.

A couple of minutes went by, and I could hear walls coming down inside the house. If they hadn't found any people, they probably wouldn't find any dope. But they were giving it the old pig try. When the worst suddenly seemed to be over, I lit a cigarette and sat up. And then:

"*Hey you,* what're you lookin' at?"

It was one of the cops from behind the car. The narc I had been watching was startled into action by his voice and flashed me his best piercing narc stare. They both came over to the window. "You hear what I said, boy? What're you lookin' at?"

"Oh, nothing, Officer, I was just——"

"You were just what? You want to get run in, huh, for obstructing the law?"

"No, sir, you see I was just driving through when——"

"I didn't ask you what you were doing, wise guy, I asked you what you were lookin' at, huh? Now you gonna answer me, or you want to double-talk the Captain down at the station?"

"No, sir."

"No sir what? What d'you mean, no sir. I asked you a question. You gonna cooperate or not?"

"Yes, sir, I certainly will."

"Then what were you lookin' at, just then?"

"Nothing, sir, I was just on the street when I heard the sirens, and I thought it was a fire so I pulled over——"

"That was a long time ago, boy, a long time ago you thought it was some fire, and I'm asking you *now!* What've you been lookin' at just now!"

"Well, sir." I was scared shitless again. The suitcase was in the car and if they picked me up it wouldn't take long for them to pick up on what was happening.

"Whatsamatter, boy, you tongue-tied? Huh? I asked you a question. You gonna answer me or not, 'cause if you're not I got other places I can ask you, understand?" Suddenly he stepped back and took a fresh look at me. "You a college boy? Is that what's wrong, huh? College boy, don't like to talk to no police, think your girl won't like you anymore, is that it? Huh?"

I decided the only way out was to kiss ass. "Yes, sir."

"Yes, sir, what?"

"Yes, sir, I am a student."

"A student. A student, huh? Oh, I beg your pardon, student. I thought you were a college boy. Well, tell me something, student, where'd you get this car, huh? Did your student studies get it for you, or what? Huh? Tell me about this car you got here."

"Well, sir, ah, my, ah . . . my father bought it for me."

"Oh, I see, your father bought it for his student."

"Yes, sir."

"When your father bought this car for his student, did he by any chance make sure that his student was a student of driving, or did he just give it to the college boy?"

"Ah, well sir, I ah——" I ah was ah scared shitless that he ah was going to ah ask me for my license. Ahhhhhhh.

"What I'm asking you, boy, in plain language that even I can understand, see, even me who never was no college graduate, what I'm asking you is if you know how to operate this vehicle."

"Yes, sir, I do."

"Well then why don't you do yourself a favor, and operate it right out of here right now!" He was almost yelling.

"Well, sir, I was going to do just that, but . . ." I pointed feebly at the massed cop-cars, which blocked the road.

"Well, then put the car in reverse, goddamn you, and git out of here!"

"Yes, sir, yes, sir, yes, sir," as I started the car up again and backed out of there as fast as I could, and at the end of the street, moving off at good speed, I leaned out and shouted "Fuck you!" as loud as I could. It didn't make much difference.

5

I was back out on the Avenue again and hot-assing it up toward the campus before I realized I was still hungry. So I pulled into the first place I saw, which was a Peter Piper. Like everything else in California, Peter Piper is designed strictly for cars. You drive up in your car, order from your car, pick up the food in the car, and then park and eat in the car.

While you wait in line—in your car—you read the large sign that tells you what Peter offers in the way of nutrition. Finally, as the line progresses, you arrive alongside a large, maniacally smiling being, who is Peter. BE READY says the sign above his head in bright neon colors, PETER WILL SPEAK TO YOU. About the time you think you're ready to punch Peter in his gleaming polished plastic snout, a thick intercom voice barks "Yeah, what'll it be?" And you tell Peter, and he repeats it back to you, grinning his fixed, idiot smile. And then you nose to the front and wait for the food.

If you can drive a car, you can go see Peter as often as you like.

6

I felt better after eating, all primed and ready to go. Where I was going to go was another question entirely. I didn't have the slightest idea what I was going to do next—all I really knew was what I couldn't do. I couldn't find Musty. I didn't know how even to begin to look for him. He was John's connection, not mine.

And I couldn't call John in Cambridge, because he had become convinced his line was tapped and had his phone taken out. I could try to reach him at Sandra's place, on the phone we always did business on, but John wouldn't be with her at this hour.

And I couldn't go back to Cambridge without scoring something, because that would be a hundred and sixty bucks in plane fare down the drain and, more important, all our timing thrown off.

Which left me with no leads, no place to crash, twenty-five hundred bucks in my sportcoat, and a connection who was probably busting ass for Mexico, unless they'd already caught up with him. Not a particularly cheerful prospect. So I just drove around Berkeley, looking for somebody I knew and trying desperately to remember a single street address out of the dozens I knew in that town. I'd spent time in Berkeley before—mostly on three-day dope trips like this one—but one trip last spring had lasted a month. It hadn't started as a month trip, but that's the way it had worked out. And I'd met a lot of good people—I'd been things and seen places, as the saying goes.

But now, just when I needed them, the addresses and names wouldn't come back, and I wound up parking the car in the municipal lot off Channing, so I could walk up to campus and look around. It was late in the day and the Avenue was jumping. The freaks were out in their usual positions: stoned hostile funky greaser freaks on the west side of Telegraph and stoned outasight panhandling peace freaks on the east side. The bikies were lined up in full formation in front of Pepe's and I could hear some pickets up on Sproul Plaza. I hurried on to see what they were putting down, forgetting that I still had on my Weejuns and jacket. That was a mistake, because I looked like I should've been up on the hill drinking keg beer with the jolly mindless frat brothers, and since I wasn't . . . The street punks jumped into action, edged toward me; all around me their soft liturgical drone filled the air: "lids, speed, acid; righteous lids" as the street people decided they had me figured. What a drag.

Up on campus a heavy scene was under way. The Berkeley police were huddled like sullen refugees under Sather Gate, looking as if they were just waiting for the word to come down swinging. And on Sproul Plaza there was a slowly circling ring of picketers, chanting and stomping. Most of them had helmets on; anyone who exercised the right to assemble and petition in this town knew what to expect.

In the center of the ring a heavy-set, shaded and leathered black man, beret tilted to one side and covered with buttons like a war hero with medals: "Brothers and Sisters, the time has come for us to act. There is no longer a defensible middle of the road. And by that I mean the middle of the road, man, that sit-on-the-fence shit. 'Cause when the long knives come"—it was not a threat, but logic—"when the long knives come, they aren't gonna ask where you stand, and where you been standin'. They're gonna know!" He was rapping and flapping his arms, talking to the picketers, turning away to speak to the crowd. Trying to get that old group-solidarity number down before the heat did. There was no middle ground, he said again, no fence left to sit on.

"You're either part of the problem or part of the solution!" He shouted at passersby, fringe observers like me. "Part of the problem or part of the solution. The time has come to act," he went on. "Join the Third World Brothers and Sisters, in support of their legitimate demands for Third World Faculty and Curriculum. And join them now."

There was a lot of energy running through the crowd, and I was suddenly uncomfortable, standing there in my Hahvud Yahd monkey suit. The lines were sharply drawn in Berkeley, and everyone understood what they meant: the fight had already begun. Nobody said you had to get on the battlefield, but then . . . it wasn't hard to put yourself in No Man's Land. I looked back at the cops, who were starting to move toward the picketers.

". . . or Donald Duck Reagan or Mickey Mouse Rafferty. And we can't relate to seeing our black brothers dying to support this pig fascist system in the rice paddies of Vietnam. We can't relate to that and we can't stand by and watch it happen no more neither. The time has come to act. Join the pickets now."

The pigs were bearing down, and I beat a hasty retreat back across the street. The pickets had picked up on the energy now, and were stamping their feet as they marched, chanting *Who* are the people, *We* are the people, *Power to the people.* Yeah. Get that ball. Fight, team, fight. Push 'em back, push 'em back, *waaaaaaaay* back. I began to think about how nobody had ever really figured out what four years of high school did to a reasonably healthy mind. Then I saw somebody I knew: Steven.

7

Stevie's place was peaceful and quiet, in the back of a house on Dwight Way. It looked onto a lot that had once been used for parking but which had, miraculously, fallen into disuse. Someone had planted a small garden and there were people all around, sitting out on their back steps, smoking dope in the sunset and laughing quietly. I remembered my dorm room in Cambridge, which had a generous view of all four lanes of Memorial Drive, complete with traffic jams twice a day, and wondered again why I hadn't transferred to Berkeley when Stevie did.

You never realize what you're missing until you come to Berkeley—and when you leave, it's easy to forget. The air is light, the sun bright, and you feel tremendously energetic and strong. You also experience a sudden resistance to credibility gaps, realities of life, overdue bills, and other pitfalls of the American way. That's why the "campus revolt" began in Berkeley, and that's why it has never made more sense than it did, and still does, in Berkeley: because the people who are striking and picketing are picking up their energy from the land. When the sun shines in that town, life is so outrageously beautiful that a black man shot in Oakland the night before, or a zillion tons of bombs dropped on Quongquong in the last week, doesn't seem wrong—it doesn't seem like anything. It is inconceivable, and totally ludicrous. Which is what it would seem like to intelligent people anywhere. The difference is that in Berkeley, at least, the need to rectify the ludicrous offense is as obvious and natural as the presence of the sun in the sky.

Even the little details show. Like in Boston, if you want to call for the exact time, you dial 637–8687, which in letters spells "nervous." In Berkeley, the equivalent number spells "popcorn."

Stevie brought out a couple of joints and a gallon of Red Mountain. He gave me a joint and then a glass, and said again that it was great to see me. Then he said, "How's Annie doing?"

"Okay," I said. The hooch was good. "Well, not okay.

I don't know. Shitty, in fact. I haven't seen her for about a month now."

"Jeez, I thought you two were really . . ."

"Yeah, well . . ." I shrugged. "I still dig her." I lit the joint. It was even better. "She's bumming around with some dipshit from the Piggy Club now. I see her every once in a while on Mt. Auburn Street, smashed out of her mind. We exchange pleasantries and that's about it. You know. How's Barbara?"

"Cool," Stevie said. "Great chick. Everything's cool." He lit his joint and said, "Came out here to get away from Annie, huh?"

I shook my head. "Not really." Stevie had introduced me to Annie about a year before, and ever since he'd taken a kind of paternal interest in how we were doing. But hell, I thought, people changed. I'd changed, she'd changed. It had been a good thing but it wasn't any more, and I didn't feel like talking about it. "Not really," I said again.

"You and your parents seeing eye-to-eye these days?" he asked.

I laughed and shook my head. I knew what he was asking. He was asking how I could afford the trip out. "Not exactly," I said.

"You dealing again?" Stevie asked, pulling a long face. "I thought you quit that."

"I did," I said, "but John's been getting into it lately. Pretty heavily, in fact. He's turning over about twenty bricks a week."

"Far out," Stevie said. "Twenty bricks a week, around Cambridge?"

"Yeah, everyone's turning on these days. But you know John. He's not particularly interested in the details, just the wheeling-dealing. So here I am."

"Just doing bricks this time?"

"Yeah. Just bricks. Ten in the little bag under my seat and away I go. With a free vacation in California in the process."

"You ought to knock that shit off," Stevie said. "You're going to get busted sometime."

I shrugged. "You drive a car long enough, you'll have an accident." I took a long hit off my joint. "Anyway, there wasn't anything else to do. I mean, this is spring break, right? So I can come out here and dig what's happening, or I can go back to fucking Westhrop to spend a restful week listening to the old man telling me what I ought to do with my life, while the old lady asks me where they've gone wrong." I laughed. "You know, man, you got a moustache and they want to know where they've gone wrong. Fuck that. If I started pushing beds across the country and organizing panty raids they'd be unhappy because I was apathetic and uninvolved. You can't win. Shit, I don't even want to win any more. I just want to do the things I want to do."

"Yeah," Stevie said, "I'm hip." He lay back on the couch and stared up at the tinted sky. We were silent for a while, and then he said, "You still buying from Ernie out here?"

I shook my head. "Ernie's not too cool these days. He got busted with thirty bricks last month and didn't have the bread to buy himself off."

"Is that right?" Stevie said, sitting up, suddenly interested. "But I just saw him last week . . ." He stopped. He thought it over. "Maybe he found somebody to post bail."

"Maybe."

He looked vaguely apprehensive. "Well, if he made a deal, he'll just turn in a couple of smack freaks." He thought that over, and then added, "He wouldn't turn in any of his friends. Ernie's all right."

"I'll let somebody else find that out," I said.

"Ernie's all right."

"Yeah, probably he is. But we've got another connection now, and there's no question about whether he's cool or not. Which reminds me, can I use your phone?"

"Yeah, sure," Stevie said. He got up, and followed me back into the kitchen. I was asking how to dial information when there was a noise at the back door and a huge freak walked in, holding his head and bleeding.

It was Ross.

8

There was blood all over everything, including the little blond chick who was holding him up. As usual, Ross had his sheepskin vest on, and as usual, he was mad. Ross was always mad about something; a good bust in the head just gave him a chance to focus his energy. He slumped down on the couch with the chick, beneath the poster that said SEE AMERICA FIRST. Stevie ran for a rag.

"What happened?" I asked the chick, who was crying and wiping her face and Ross's with the same bloody handkerchief. There was a hell of a lot of blood, but then Ross was a hell of a big boy. He was big enough to be playing football for Ohio State, except that this was Berkeley, and Ross had hair down to his shoulders and was wearing a huge pair of yellow shades. One frame was shattered and they were lopsided on his nose now as he looked up at me.

"Oh," he said. "It's you."

"What happened?" I said again.

"Up on campus," the chick said, "the Governor gave the order to the pigs to break up the picket lines." I tilted my head. "We were keeping people from classes," she added.

"At seven o'clock at night," Ross said. "The motherfuckers, keeping people from classes at seven at night."

"So the pigs broke it up," the chick said. She had stopped crying and was staring at my clothes. Stevie came back with a rag and started wiping more blood off Ross's face. "Motherfuckers," Ross kept saying.

"Quit moving your head," said Stevie.

"See it now," Ross said, to no one in particular. Suddenly he tilted his nose in the air and started sniffing. Sniff, sniff. "Goddamn," he suddenly said. "Goddamn morons. You been smoking again."

"Relax," Stevie said.

"Goddamn," Ross said, "now of all times."

Stevie and the chick were working on him. Stevie said to her, "Sukie, this is Peter. Peter, Sukie."

"Hello," Sukie said. Her back was to me. She was bent over Ross, putting merthiolate on his head. Her long legs were stretched taut, and they were very brown. Hello, hello.

"You guys are going to screw everything," Ross said. "You're going to get us all busted for sure. Jesus, I think if you have too much of this, it begins to affect your brains. I think——"

"Quit moving your head," Stevie said again. He glanced over at me and we exchanged looks. Old Ross. He'd never change.

He sat patiently until they had patched up his head, then stumbled off to the bathroom, with the chick still supporting him. When they'd gone, Stevie said, "He bought another one."

"Oh?" Nothing had changed since the year before.

"Yeah. Last week."

"What was it?"

"Shotgun," Stevie said.

"Out of sight. What's he got lying around by now?"

"I don't know. At least six. Two shotguns for sure."

"Two?"

"Yeah, one to replace the automatic. He jammed it last week and he's having a hard time getting it fixed."

I nodded. Seeing as how automatics were illegal, you'd have a very hard time getting one fixed. Besides the fact that none of Ross's guns was registered. But that was the way his head worked. He figured that if he registered his guns, he'd just be tipping them off—the big "them"—so that when the day of liberation came they would know about him, would know to come and get him. He figured that they probably already knew enough about him to come and get him anyway, but just let them try. He was ready. Muthafuggin' pigs.

It probably would have been a cool idea for Ross to keep his guns out of sight if he'd been doing anything, if he'd been a Panther or a Weatherman—even if he'd been a member of the Sierra Club. Anything. But Ross wasn't doing anything, short of letting everyone know what a heavy he was, and knocking out a few token Bank of America windows with the butt of his gun when the inevitable spring riot came to Berkeley. That was why he always cut such a ludicrous figure to me.

Ross was a fervent Marxist-Leninist. At least, that's how he thought of himself. He was one of the first people I'd ever met in Berkeley. I'd just been walking down Telegraph, digging the street scene, and he'd looked like he knew his way around, so I'd asked him if he knew where such-and-such Dwight Way was. He lived there too.

We'd been great good friends for an hour or so, which was, I later discovered, about as long as Rossie could function before finding it necessary to pause and consider the state of the coming revolution. So we'd started talking about the revolution, and after a bit of it I'd just laughed—and that had offended him deeply. You could do anything, say anything, be anything, to Ross—but you couldn't laugh at the revolution.

Later, when Stevie mentioned that I was in Berkeley to score some dope, the dislike had turned to contempt. Ross had no place in his life for drugs. He was serious enough about his trip to live in constant preparedness for the big day. He didn't drink, he didn't smoke, and you could hear him panting every night as he did his calisthenics. He stayed in shape for it, and he expected others to do the same. And so he especially detested dope people, whose presence meant a possible bust, and with it the confiscation of his well-maintained arsenal. We really didn't get along.

But what bothered me about Ross, in the end, was that he couldn't dig what anybody else was up to. I mean, I didn't want the dude to knock off what he was doing just because I couldn't dig it, but that was exactly what he seemed to want me to do. And as far as I was concerned, that was half-assed, because it all came down to personal excuses, which were purely a matter of choice. His excuse for not paying any attention to us was that we blew dope, which was not only illegal but was quite literally an opiate of the people, an anti-revolutionary device that we were politically ignorant enough to indulge in.

And our excuse for not digging Ross's trip was that we figured that any changes that were really going to happen were going to happen in people's heads. We figured that once you started killing, you admitted that you were at a loss for other solutions, and that your own way was so poverty-stricken in the knowledge department that all you could do with people who didn't see the light was liquidate them. And we figured that was nowhere. So we blew our dope and stayed in our heads; maybe that was nowhere, but that was our problem.

The only hitch in all this was that, from the point of view of Ross's repressionary society, he was a lot cooler than we were. I mean some places the written penalties for selling marijuana are greater than the written penalties for killing somebody. In that sense, Ross was a lot more hip than we were.

9

Stevie and I sat in the living room, waiting for something to happen. Pretty soon the chick came back out. I was fumbling around for a cigarette, but I didn't have a match. "Do you have a match?" I asked her.

She stared at me blandly for a moment, then said, "If you made a salad out of tobacco leaves and ate it, you would be very sick." It was said without judgment or heat, simply a stated fact. But all I could think was, Christ, not again. Another California health-food freak.

"Stevie, got a match?"

He shook his head. "I'm all out, man. Ask Ross, why don't you."

Just then Ross came out of the bathroom, still holding a towel to his head. He was mumbling to himself, so I left the honors to Stevie.

"Ross, you got a match?" he asked.

"So you can smoke some more dope and stink the place up? Hell, no."

"It's not for a joint," said Stevie. "Just a plain, ordinary butt that won't stink anything up any more than it already is. For Peter," he added.

"Okay," he said. "Okay. In my room, near the phone." As I got up he said, "Hey, and there's a number by the phone that you were supposed to call if you showed up here. Some guy from Boston called this morning and left it."

I nodded and said, "Thanks."

"If you call Boston, call collect," Ross yelled after me as I went into his room.

There was a number with a Boston exchange written on a newspaper. There was blood all over the paper and I wasn't sure of the last digit, but what the hell. I dialed and a far-off voice answered.

"Hello?"

"This is Peter," I said.

"Oh, yeah," said John. He sounded like I had just wakened him, which was the way he always sounded on the telephone. "What's happening?"

"Not much. I got invited to a bust but I didn't attend."

"Good man. Musty gave me a ring about five hours ago. He said he'd had to split his place fast."

"No kidding," I said.

John ignored me. "Yeah. We were really worried about you for a while there, Peter." I'll bet he was. It would've cost him a lot of bread. As if he knew what I was thinking, John went on. "We were afraid the heat might hassle you when they found the house clean."

I said, "They did. Big deal."

"Ummm." I had half expected congratulations on my narrow escape, but of course there weren't any. John said, "Big bust?"

"Eight narcs. Couple of patrol cars."

"Shit, that's the trouble with Musty. When they come down on him, they come down hard."

"I thought he was so cool," I said.

"For Chrissake," said John, "he is. He knew this was coming. He called me, didn't he? Don't worry about it."

"Okay," I said, "okay. You know where he is now?"

"Just a minute." John left the phone. I could hear music in the background and, faintly, a chick giggling. Then John came back. "Peter?" he said. "Take this number down." He gave me an Oakland number, told me to be careful, and hung up. I sighed a deep sigh of relief, knowing at last that everything was still cool. I felt like I could relax a bit, maybe even dig the Sukie chick for a while before I dived back into the business routine. I picked up Ross's matches and went back into the living room.

Ross was sitting alone on the couch, smiling and drinking a medicinal glass of wine. He was telling Stevie with great glee how he'd managed to kick a cop in the 'nads before they'd gotten to him. "Took that fucking pig right out with me," he said.

Stevie looked up at me. "Everything okay?" he asked.

"Yeah, fine," I said. "Thanks." Then to Ross: "Where's your old lady?"

"Who, you mean Sukie?" I nodded, and he laughed. "She's not my old lady, man. Just a good head. She hangs around to take care of friends on days like this, when she knows there's going to be trouble."

"Where'd she go?" I asked.

"She went back up to campus to see what's happening." He looked at me hard, and then laughed again. "You can forget about her, Harkness, if you're thinking what I think you're thinking. She's got a good head. She doesn't go for druggies like you."

"Oh, I see," I said.

"What's that supposed to mean?" he asked, but I just shook my head and sat down. I wasn't going to argue with the dude, I was just going to relax for a change and enjoy myself. In my hand I had the number John had given me, Musty's number. I should've been on the phone trying to get hold of him, to set up a time. But I didn't feel like I had to be in any rush. I could wait. Musty had almost put me on the shithook, and it was my turn to reciprocate. He could sweat it for a while, not knowing whether I'd been picked up. It was all part of the game.

10

Dealing is funny, as a game. It is very external and controlled and it follows patterns of protocol and consequences as rigid as any ever encountered by Nine-to-Five Man. More rigid, perhaps, since not everyone is playing the dealing game on the same scale, or with the same intensity, or with the same degree of knowledge.

But everyone in the park is playing, whether he's on the grass or in the bleachers drinking beer, because everyone figures he's got something to lose. Essentially, that is what makes dealing so dangerous and so thrilling —the simple fact that everyone is convinced he's got something to lose. Because not everyone is going to admit it.

That's the difference between the dealer and Nine-to-Five Man, who is forced to admit it, whether he likes it or not. He has to wear a suit to work, and he has to keep his shoes shined, and he has to get haircuts and watch out for tell-tale underarm stains. These rules are accepted by J. P. Nine-to-Five, by Mrs. Ruth Wanamaker Nine-to-Five, and by all the little Nine-to-Fives. It's accepted by them and before they know it, it is them, for which they receive the Consolation Prize of Knowing Who They Are. And everybody's happy so long as the supply of glycerin suppositories holds out.

But that's not what's happening on the street, because all the people who are playing there aren't sure they're playing, and sometimes they're most definitely not playing but only trying to play, or thinking they want to play, or some variation thereof. That's what makes dealing so interesting.

It doesn't start that way, of course, with the fully developed patterns and responses and the paranoia and the inimitable thrills and chills. It usually starts as an act of love and only later turns into a game.

You start with John Joseph Straight, single, on his way through life with one finger cocked piously up his ass and another thumbing through the Yellow Pages. To this sturdy fellow add two Pernicious Influences, one Psychedelic Experience, a taste of rock 'n' roll music, and some form or another of Idle Mind (which is widely accepted as the Devil's Playground). Beat Pernicious Influences and Psychedelic Experience until fluffy, add rock 'n' roll, season with Idle Mind, and lick the gummed side. Hold a match to one end, insert in mouth. You are now smoking a joint and wondering why you never thought to do this before, while the little man in the back of your head who holds the keys to your future is rolling around on the medulla in a fit of epilepsy. He is shouting that you will never be the same again, that you have permanently damaged your chromosomes and your taste buds, and that you have generally corrupted your body and fulfilled your parents' Worst Expectations. That is, that's what he would be saying if you could hear him. But right now you are thinking you have never in your whole life ever noticed how perfidiously intricate the sun looks coming through a half-filled cut-glass decanter of wine, or how amusing it is that your belly button should be stopped shut, while your nose has two holes instead of one.

After a few experiences of this sort, the dastardly weed becomes a fond and coveted friend, and it attracts others. That is to say, in the spirit of brotherhood and togetherness which is the mark of the Aquarian Age, you and your friends blow grass together; and those of your friends who don't aren't around much any more. This isn't any fault of yours—you're still digging them as much as you did before—but you just can't stand those soon-to-be-behind-bars looks they give you when you get your shit out and ask them if they want a smoke; or the way they ask you if you're high on "that stuff" before they'll tell you how ugly their date was last night.

So you and your dope friends blow dope together, and have a lot of good times together, and watch the sun go down every night together, and go to Baskin-Robbins to taste ice cream together. And after a while it gets so that you're blowing a *lot* of dope together.

And that's cool, contrary to the local witch doctor's medicinal meditations or the Surgeon General's latest case of the blahs. Because you know—having violated the number-one principle of Western science and entered into self-experimentation—you know that dope doesn't make your eyes bug out, or make your head split open and grow asparagus. And you know that you don't wake up the morning after with the cold-turkey, liver-lidded, hungry, frenzied, glassy-eyed, pure *need* look of *dope* in your eyes, because you're eating better and sleeping more than you ever have before. And you know that grass doesn't zap your brain into the fourth dimension only to drop it off in the second, leaving you with three eyes and a dork the size of a pineapple and the insistent, insane, uncontrollable need to kill, rape, pillage, and plunder (which a stint in the army would at least teach you how to do)—because in that sense grass is very uneducational.

On the contrary, you find that it is vocational. You change your name to Phineas Phreak or Seymour Stone, and wear bellbottoms and dirty BVDs and grow your hair down to your ass and try to keep from passing Go while still collecting your two hundred bucks for tuition every month. You cancel your subscription to *The New York Times* and read the L.A. *Free Press* and don't brush your teeth and look sullen as much as possible. You hang up when old girl friends call and lead a mysteriously quiet life, enjoying the knowledge that your straight friends are worrying about your health and the "deterioration of his nervous system."

But most of all you become conscious of the extent to which you were hoaxed by people you once believed in: dope doesn't drive you to needles or crime, and you still laugh at your father's dull jokes.

So you try to create your own mechanism, and struggle to survive within it. You do what you think is right, and you say not what you're supposed to say, usually not even what you want to say, but what you have to say. And then one morning you wake up and it's you they're describing in the editorials, and they're talking about you like you're a piece of shit that won't flush. You've dropped out, it seems. You're alienated and God knows what else.

By this time, however, your evil habit is consuming a bit more of your lunch money than it properly should, and you and your friends decide to start buying in quantity. This makes for cheaper dope and, quite often, for better dope, because you're getting a solid chunk of a brick, and not a lid bag half full of oregano. So you find a big dealer and buy stuff for your friends, and they love you for being so wise in the ways of the street and so kind to their pockets and throats.

Which continues until you finally realize, one day, that you don't have to pay for any of your smoking dope if you buy in quantity with your friends and then sell a few ounces at street prices to anybody who's interested. And probably by this time your parents have seen a picture of you in the papers with long hair, hanging out of the occupied administration building, and they have told you to come home to Flat Top Community College or be damned—which is to say, you have been cut off. So that's the way it begins, with a few lids to friends to keep the bookstore off your back, or the landlord or the used-car salesman or whoever else has it in for you at the time, and from there it grows like a weed. And soon enough you're dealing quite a bit of dope and you aren't seeing many friends, since you're either buying or selling or smoking with buyers or sellers, and you spend a lot of time hustling and being far out and saying, "Oh, *wow!* Hey man, did you *dig* that?" And it goes on that way for as long as you can stand it—forever, if you can stand it that long. But the chances are good that the game will grow either too bold or too old, and the routines too sadly and forlornly familiar, and you will retire from street life and go back to where you came from. Which is where you are.

11

I called Musty's number in Oakland and some guy who seemed to know said I should come over, that everything was cool. I was supposed to ring the buzzer under Carol Moss. I said fine and went over.

Driving over in the car, I felt better and better. It was a beautiful spring night and the windows were down; I could hear the sounds of the street and the people. The driving was mechanical and I began to drift into the fantasy, the current fantasy you might call it, but strong just the same. At first it was just faces: faces in my mind, faces of the people blurring as I drove past them, and then I saw the crowd fanned out before me like a huge faceless corpse, dead but alive, jumping and jiving as I tuned up for the next number, and I was telling the engineers to make sure all the recording equipment was in order, because I didn't want to have to do it more than once. If I had things my way I was going to do the damn thing once and then get out from under the glaring heat of those spots, out into the night and away. They yelled back that everything was cool and I nodded to Willie. He thumped up the bass and started it rolling, drifting and flowing, echoing hollow from the P.A. speakers in the back of the stadium. And then the drums chopped in, stomping and humping, with the light clang of the cymbals on top of it, and then we were into it, the crowd knew that it was what they'd been waiting for all night and they moaned, an insane screaming moan of pleasure, screaming, *We love it, it's yours, it's yours, we love it, we love it.* And then the harp flew in and we were going, man, we were going and this was all they were going to get, but before we went they were going to get it. Just then the cords broke in front of the stage and there were cops all over the place, tripping and falling over the equipment and themselves and the chicks clawing and grasping and then it was gone, done and gone, and the MC was yelling "The New Administration," and the crowd was chanting for more, more, but we were down and under and out of the lights . . .

The lights, Jesus, I'd just run a red light and some poor bastard back there was screaming at me. I checked the rear-view mirror nervously, but there was no heat. Pure luck. I took a deep breath and there were no more faces. I finished the drive and parked across from the address I had been given.

It was an old, two-story house with big bay windows. There was a chopped Harley leaning against the side of the house, back behind the cars so you couldn't see it easily from the road; it must be Musty's. I smiled in the darkness. Connection at last.

I pressed the buzzer and a funky little blonde showed up, wearing a bathrobe that was much too big for her and an irritated expression. She sized me up with a cold eye, like one of those people at fairs who guess how much you weigh. "You're the guy from the Coast," she said. "In the back."

I stepped into the hallway, which smelled old and dark. "Are you Carol Moss?" I said. "I'm——"

"In the back," she said, walking away.

The hall led me back toward the only light in the place, past the stairs leading up to the second floor, past an empty living room and a foul-smelling can. I came out into the light and saw three dudes sitting around a small kitchen table. There was a nappy-looking spade in a white linen suit, a guy with long curly hair and a droopy moustache, and a little guy with glasses and a nervous look. They all glanced up when I came in, but went right on talking.

"Last night," said the little guy with tiny pupils and glasses, "last night was heaven. It was just heaven! I didn't think twice about it all day, just went in when I felt it coming and bingo! dropped it clean as a whistle."

"Was it tapered at the end, like a fine cigar?" the spade asked.

"No," the little guy said. He got a suspicious look. "Why do you ask?"

"You should make sure it's tapered," he said. "So your ass won't slam shut." He laughed at that, and the dude with the moustache laughed too. The little guy looked annoyed.

"No," he said, "it wasn't tapered. No, it wasn't." He began to smile at the recollection. "As a matter of fact, perfectly round and hard, and what a relief! What pleasure! I mean it was just——"

"Heaven," Moustache said. "You told us once before." Moustache seemed a little bored with the conversation. He looked up at me. "You Harkness?"

"Yeah."

"Have a seat," he said. "You're just in time to hear Lou tell us all about his intestines. This is Lou," he said, pointing to the little guy, "and Clarence. I'm Musty."

I nodded, they nodded, and I sat down. Lou looked spiteful. There was only a bare bulb overhead, and the walls were painted black, giving the placc a séance atmosphere. The walls were covered with posters: Peter Fonda on a hog, with a sign saying OURS IS THE ADDICTED SOCIETY; Jimi Hendrix scratching his belly; Bill Miller for Berkeley City Council. They didn't have the one of Frank Zappa on the can, I thought. But then, they did have Lou.

Lou sensed a lull in the conversation and was off again, full speed ahead. "You know," he said, "today's been just awful. I mean, really awful. That bust on Holly Street's left me tighter than a miser. I've tried three times since dinner . . ." he held his hands out wide, as if to show they were clean ". . . and nothing. Nothing!"

"You need a systems analysis," Clarence said, and laughed.

Lou was wide-eyed serious. "You think so? Does that help?"

"Cut the shit, Lou," said Musty. He turned to me. "Good trip?"

"Little dull so far," I said, lighting a cigarette. Nobody laughed.

"You miss the bust?" I shrugged. Obviously, I had missed the goddamn bust. "Sorry that happened," Musty said. But, like John, he didn't seem very concerned. "How's John?"

"Fine, he's fine."

"Well," Musty said, "we got your stuff here. It's not quite Michoacán, but it's nice. Very smooth." He pointed over beside the stove, where there were a lot of bricks wrapped in foil. "Very nice gold," he said. "John'll really dig it."

Then we talked about the bust for a while. Clarence asked me how the heat was in Boston.

"About usual," I said. "They don't hassle the colleges much. Mostly they try to hit you when you're away from the nest. Airports, stuff like that."

"I think . . ." Lou began.

"That sucks," Musty said, "that airport thing. You want these bricks now?"

"I think . . ." Lou said, a grin beginning.

"No," I said. "Cat I'm staying with doesn't want any dope at his place. He's got a paranoid friend."

"I think it's coming!" Lou yelled, jumping up from the table and running down the hall to the can.

"You got a place to stay?" Musty asked.

"Yeah, for tonight at least. I might be around later in the week, though. Could you put me up here?"

"No problem. There's a room upstairs that's empty, Jack's room. You can use that. And the place'll be cool because I'm going to get these bricks out of here for a while. When are you leaving?"

"Goddammit, where's the toilet paper?" came a muffled voice from the can.

"Monday," I said.

"Okay. We'll have the dope for you before you go."

Carol Moss walked into the kitchen, poured herself a glass of milk, and walked out without saying a word.

"What's hassling her?"

"Me," Musty said, laughing. "She's ripped at me because I spend more time with my machine than I do with her. You see my hog out there when you came up to the house?" I nodded. "Fine machine. That's a fine fucking machine. I keep telling her that if she had seventy-four cubic inches I'd spend more time riding her, but she doesn't think that's so funny."

"No sense of humor, huh?" I said. They didn't think that was so funny either.

"You could say that," Musty said.

"I gotta split," Clarence said, standing up, "before Lou comes back to tell us how it was." He nodded to Musty and said to me, "Catch you later, man," and was gone.

Lou returned, looking ecstatic. "Boy you shoulda seen——"

"You want to taste it?" asked Musty, nodding over at the bricks.

"Sure," I said.

"Listen," Lou said, sitting down with us. "Listen, guys, yesterday was nothing compared to the one I just dropped."

Musty suddenly turned on Lou. "Why don't you just forget about your bowels for a while?"

Lou looked hurt. "What's the matter with you? Just 'cause you almost got your ass busted today doesn't mean I have to——"

"Just shut up," Musty said. "I don't feel like hearing about it any more, and I'm sure Harkness here doesn't either."

Lou looked over at me, defensively. "You don't like hearing about it?" he demanded. I shrugged.

"Look, Lou," said Musty, suddenly smiling. "Why don't you go for a nice long walk. The air'd do you good, you've told me that it does you good a million times."

Lou looked sour. Finally he said, "Okay, I'll go. But I'm not walking. Give me the keys to your wheels."

Musty laughed. "Haven't got the wheels here," he said. "Too hot. I left them in the garage down by the Holly Street place. And I'm sure as hell not giving you my bike, if that's what you're thinking about. Nobody drives my bike. Except me." There was a silence, while Lou looked glum and Musty laughed some more. Then he said, "What about you?" I realized he was talking to me. "How about it, Harkness? Did you drive over?"

"Yeah," I said, trying to sound noncommittal. I wasn't too big on giving the car to some dude I didn't know from a hole in the ground.

"Well," Musty went on, "Lou here is cool. Aren't you, Lou?" Lou nodded. I was thinking just then that I'd hang around for a while and taste the dope, so what the hell. "Come back soon," I said, pulling out the keys. "And just don't bust it up, okay? It's not my car." We all laughed and Lou hustled out the door.

"He's a weird little dude," I said, but Musty was already over in the corner, opening one of the bricks. He removed the tin foil first, then the paper wrapping. On the paper was a peace sign and the words BERKELEY 890. I wondered what it meant and then realized it must be the gram weight—not a bad one at that. A righteous brick, eight hundred ninety grams. Below that was a large, stenciled *M*. Musty saw me looking at it and laughed.

"My trademark," he said. "I wanted to get one of those hand-press stampers, so I could punch it right into the brick. But, shit, you know what they want for those things?"

"No," I said, thinking that Musty was pretty cocky. Or else pretty fucking good.

"Like a thousand bucks, man. I looked into it."

It was cocky, but it wasn't unheard of, trademarking your own dope. A lot of dudes had done it, most notably Augustus Stanley Owsley III, who'd helped put acid in the dictionary. He used to stamp a little owl right into his tabs; it was like the Good Housekeeping Seal of Approval. It meant that the acid was pure, with a good base and a uniform three-hundred-five-mic dose. It also meant another two bucks a tab on the street.

Musty pulled a hunk off one of the bricks, and began rolling some joints. While he rolled he talked about the dope supply, the way things were getting tight. "It's the same all over the country," he said. "Christ. Used to be a year-round business, now it's getting seasonal. It's only April now, and the squeeze is on already. Everybody's cracking down."

"Cracking down?" I said. "Dealers, or what?"

"Well, dealers, yeah, but mainly it's the full-scale crackdowns that hurt. Like the American government leans on the Mexicans, and the Mexes, dumb fuckers, start burning crops. And then the border guards start getting honest and the FBI decides to do nothing but hassle big runners—and things get tight."

"Shit," I said. "The FBI? Haven't they got better things to do?"

"Never have before," Musty said. "Old J. Edgar and the boys have been mowing down straw men for years—communists, dope fiends, hidden persuaders, anything they can think of. Anything that sounds tough but can't fight back. They're smart, man. If they didn't keep everybody hopped up about the red menace and the international dope conspiracy, then they'd have to really get down to work and do something. Like go after the mob—and the mob's a tough cookie, man. The mob'd bust J. Edgar's balls." He sighed, finished one joint, licked it, set it aside, and started on another. "Listen," he said, "you know why the mob doesn't deal dope—and why the only people who get busted by the FBI are punk pushers like me? You know why? Because the mob doesn't want anything to do with grass. They're not interested. Grass is small-time, and it's too bulky to move without a lot of hassle. But mainly they're not interested because there's no real money in it. Like a dude can smoke dope his whole life, and if the supply gets cut off it won't hassle him to stop smoking. Or if somebody's fucking the market and the price goes up, he can stop smoking. Or if the stuff he's getting is cut with milk sugar or oregano or whatever, he can stop smoking, and wait till something better comes along. 'Cause your basic teahead isn't hooked, dig, he hasn't got a monkey on his back. He's blowing his weed 'cause he digs it, period. If things get too hot, or too expensive—zap! No dope market." I nodded. Big deal. But Musty was getting into it.

"Now you figure this," he said. "The mob doesn't go for dope at all, see, because they're a business organization, out to make money. They're interested in shit that gives you a habit, creates a real market. A market that stays to buy whether the shit is only ten percent potency, or whether the price jumps five-hundred percent after the first week of supply. A market that stays no matter what, a market of guys who'll do anything they have to do to keep getting their daily fix. But the FBI isn't working on that market, see. They're out busting dope fiend creeps like me who turn innocent teeners on to a stick of mary jane every now and then."

"Far out," I said. There was nothing else to say. I had heard it all before. Anybody who was into dealing had heard it all before.

"Goddamn right it's far out," Musty said. "It's also a drag to talk about." He paused and I hoped he was through, but he suddenly picked up again. "And I'll tell you what else is a drag," he said. "A real bummer this is, too. You got any idea how many people are blowing dope these days?" I shrugged. "A hell of a lot, man," he said. "A hell of a lot. Ten or twenty million, if you read *Life* magazine. Five percent of this country, bare minimum. You have any idea how much dope all those people consume?" I shook my head. He shook his head back. "A hell of a lot, man," he said again. "And I'll tell you what happens. The heat, see, the heat figure they gotta stop all these people from blowing dope, 'cause otherwise they're going to have a country full of drug addicts on their hands, right? Right. Okay, so they crack down on the dope supply, they make it hard as hell for a normal Joe to get his hands on some normal smoking dope. And they figure that's good, see, they're doing their job and preventing everybody from getting addicted. Right?" He laughed bitterly. "But then look what happens. There's not enough dope around, so the shitbird dealers start burning the scene down. And they don't have any more good weed than the next man, so they sell shit—any kind of shit—and they cut it with something to give it a kick. And the people who know what weed's all about, see, they're not getting burned, 'cause they know better. But the people who don't know better, they get screwed."

He threw his hands up, then rapped the table once more. He was getting pretty excited. "Like these dudes who try to sell you a lid and say, 'Drink it as tea'—all that means is that they're pushing some ragweed cut with meth, and you aren't going to buy their crummy lid, right? Right. You know that, and I know that. But some high school punk isn't gonna know that, and he's gonna go home and fix himself up some tea, and if he does it often enough he's gonna have a speed habit. Too much, huh? This country has a potential drug nightmare on its hands, and the pigs are busting their balls to keep it going. All the time telling the straight mommies and daddies what a good job they're doing, keeping dope out of the kiddies' hands, when actually they're responsible for hooking more little ignorant brats on more kinds of shit than you can even think of. It's too much."

He sighed, and seemed to run out of steam. He sat

back in his chair, shaking his head, then seemed to remember the joints he had rolled. He lit one and took a drag, then handed it to me. "Comes on nice," he said. "Just wait."

Carol Moss appeared out of nowhere and sat down at the table. She didn't say anything, just sat.

"Want some smoke?" I said to her, holding out the joint. She shook her head and Musty laughed.

"Forget about her," he said. "She'll snap out of it."

I took another long, luxurious hit and then held the joint away from me, observing the fine blue-gray smoke and the creeping advance of the burning tip across the yellow terrain. And realized that I was stoned. "Wow."

Musty said, "Fine smoke, what?"

12

It was definitely extraordinary smoke, and I couldn't say a thing for a while. The events of the day got up and introduced themselves to me formally and asked me to sit and chat. Having no alternative, that is exactly what I did. It had been quite a day.

I realized that I was very tired and that the business end of everything had been concluded. I could crash. The feeling came over me like a huge breath of hot air, not uncomfortable but impossible to escape, and I knew that I wanted to sleep.

Musty was in front of me saying something. I think he was still talking about how good the dope was. My ears focused and zoomed in on his words. People talk too much, I was thinking. And they eat too much. So they fart a lot and have jizzy friends like Lou. They're fat and they drive fast cars and listen to the news and beat off to Lawrence Welk. They're lonely. They get cancer and diarrhea and heartburn and dysentery and malaria and syphilis and an education, all from talking too much. The hell with them. I wanted to go to sleep.

"Where's Lou?" I asked, and everyone in the kitchen stirred audibly.

"He said something," said Musty.

"Jesus Christ, he's alive." A chick's voice. Must be that Carol what's-her-name.

"And he wants to go to sleep!" said Musty, laughing.

"Where's Lou?" I said again. "Got to get some sleep. Completely whacked out. That dope is unbelievable."

"He's functioning," said Musty to the chick. "But just barely." Then to me: "Tell you the truth, I don't have the slightest idea where Lou is right now, and he probably doesn't either. He may be back in an hour, which was an hour ago, but it's more likely that he'll be back sometime tomorrow. He's got an old lady in North Berkeley and once he's up there he doesn't show for a while. So you might as well crash here."

"Fine," I said, "anywhere. Sorry to be so lively, but this happens to me every so often, just comes over me. Nothing I can do about it. Uncontrollable desire to close my eyes. Strange but true."

"You can take Jack's room," said Musty. "Second door on the left, at the top of the stairs. There's a sleeping bag in the closet if there aren't enough blankets."

I thanked him and split.

13

Second door on the left, open, I stumbled in. Sat down and with a sigh of relief, took off my shoes and was just about to throw off the jacket when I heard someone say "Hello." I whirled around, and there she was, or rather there it was, a shift of swirling colors so bright they hurt my eyes, glistening white teeth, beautiful tanned skin —a fine woman, the whole thing extremely fine, too fine to be true, in fact too fine to be true anytime but now. All I could think was, Please would you . . . please just go away.

"Hello," I said. I put my shoes back on and stood up. "Sorry, but they told me downstairs this room was empty. Which room is Jack's?"

"Sit down," she said, still smiling.

"I'd like to very much," I said, "in the morning. But right now I'm very sleepy and have to go to bed. So if you'd tell me where——"

"This is Jack's room," she said. "My dog is having puppies in my room and the smell is too much, and I didn't know anyone was staying here tonight, so . . ." She shrugged. "But if it really bothers you I'll leave. The smell's not *that* bad." Another beautiful smile. I was being hustled; she knew damned well I wasn't going to throw her out if her dog was having puppies. Well, hell, I figured I could probably get her to drop one of the Seconals I had with me, so the light wouldn't be on all night. I wondered how long I was going to have to be sociable before I could shove one down her throat. There was nothing to do but sit down and find out.

"Your dog's having puppies?" I said.

"Yeah," she laughed. "Six the last time I looked, but probably more by now. I'd take you in to show you, but Dagoo is getting motherly already and she wouldn't like having anybody around she didn't already know." I nodded, cursing myself for not having been born a dog, with the same prerogative. "Want to hear some sounds?" she said, and without waiting for an answer she went over to the stereo in the corner of the room. As she did she brushed her long blond hair back from her face and I saw it clearly for the first time in the candlelight. Then she came back over and sat down next to me.

"Want to smoke some dope?" she said. "Out-of-sight stuff, Musty got it for a rich friend of his back East." She produced a lid and began rolling some joints. She lit one, and placed the others in the marvelous cleft peeking over the top of her shift.

"Great place to keep your stash," I laughed. Maybe I would blow some dope. This was obviously going to take some time, this social bit.

"Got into the habit this summer, during the riots," she said. "They were hassling people just for being on the street, stopping you and frisking you for dope, anything. The cops love to give a chick a good going over, but they never check there."

I nodded and took a long hit, noticing as I did that the dope was different from the stuff I'd been tasting with Musty. And had a quick paranoid flash: was he pushing me one brick of good dope and giving me another nine keys of shit? But then I thought, No, not Musty. He was a businessman, and besides he was too close to John. No, that was the kind of stunt that smacked-out old Ernie Statler would've pulled. I laughed at the thought of Ernie, and just then a lightning bolt zinged between my ears and caressed the backs of my eyeballs. I was a new man.

"Fine smoke," I said, giving her the joint. "Very fine smoke."

"I should hope so, if you're going to knock off that much of it in one drag. Man, the look in your eyes was golden. What'sa matter, you feeling bad when I came in?"

"Just tired," I said. "It's been a long day."

"Yeah, I know what you mean," she said. "This stuff really gives you a run for your money." Then she hopped up—"Wow, listen to that!"—and went over to turn up the stereo.

She came back and sat down again and stared at me. Not really at me, but at what I was wearing. As if to say, I like you and all, but whoever told you to put those things on? I got a flash on Sproul Plaza that afternoon and suddenly realized what had been happening that day, all day, ever since I'd gotten into town. I'd been swimming upstream the whole time, because of the way I looked.

I laughed and said, "I know. Who's my tailor."

She shook her head. "No, no, I didn't mean that. It's just that, well, I just can't get over those duds. You are the one from Cambridge, aren't you?" I nodded, and she laughed. "God, do all the dope people in the East look like you?"

The way she said it, I had to laugh with her. "No, just the ones who run bricks for paranoid friends. I look like this whenever I come out here. It's a trip, huh?"

She laughed again, then said in a surprised voice, "Hey, I know where I've seen you. You were over at Steven's this afternoon."

"Yeah."

"Good friends with Steven?"

"You good friends with Ross?"

She looked at me, then shrugged. "Ross's okay. You've just got to get to know him. As a matter of fact, I remember him saying something about you. Sounded like you and him didn't get to know each other the right way."

"What is the right way?"

She laughed. "There isn't. Want another smoke?" I nodded and she reached down into her shift to retrieve another joint. I figured that at the rate we were going, neither of us would be needing a Seconal. We'd be out cold in an hour.

"This dope almost never got here today," she went on. "Musty's place got busted about ten minutes after he got the word and he barely had time to move it all out." Her eyes got big. "They wouldn't have had to bust him, either. Just his bricks. He's gotten cocky lately, and that house was rented in his own name."

"Yeah, I saw that." She stopped fumbling with the matches and looked at me. "I flew in this afternoon, see, and I only had that one address. And nobody left a note on the door."

She laughed. "Wow, I heard they took the walls out."

I nodded. "Yeah, they did. But hell, it's over, done. So why don't you light that joint."

She did, and passed it over. Then she said, "You flew out just to pick up the bricks?"

I held up my fingers. "Three days, and I'm off again."

She was incredulous. "Three days? That's all the time you're going to stay? Why not hang around, once you're out here?"

"Well, I'd like to, but I've got to get back. Exams." I laughed. "Anyway, it's not as ridiculous as it sounds, if you've ever spent a winter in Beantown." I looked at her, and she shook her head. "Oh, well, you've missed something. Snow, sleet, wind, gunk—Boston's got it all. It's a winter wonderland."

"Far out," she said. "I moved up here to get away from too much good weather. From L.A., just south of L.A., actually. Bright sun and eighty degrees all year round. It drove me nuts. So I split school and wound up here in Berkeley." She leaned close to me and gave me what was by this time a darkly stained roach. "How'd you know Musty?" she said.

"I didn't," I said. "He's a friend of a friend—that rich guy you were talking about before—dude named John. Very nice cat who unfortunately was born with a trust fund in his mouth." Then I shook my head. "That's just a state of mind," I said. "He's actually a great guy."

"Yeah," she said. "He sounds it." And as soon as I heard her say that I knew that, somehow, she'd felt the same vibrations that I had. It was John, and the world he'd built up around him: distant, alien, and totally destructive to the atmosphere in the room.

And then she was saying something about another joint and I was nodding, not thinking about that but rather about the way I was feeling, the way I was slipping and sliding head over heels into the old I-am-you-and-who-is-he? routine.

Because suddenly the old Subterranean Laundry Man was there, pulling out the dirty linen for all to see and admire, watching everything that I did. Scrutinizing idiosyncrasies, scribbling notes, making points. She has her hand on your wrist, my boy, aren't you going to respond? She trusts you and wants you, old chap, aren't you going to help the lady out? It was weird, that feeling. And it made me very nervous. I was split in two, cut down the middle, the one half watching and the other half acting on dictation. I was suddenly being careful. Careful not to blow the scene, careful not to mess up all the good work done so far, careful to keep the emotional strain to a minimum until I could manage to plunk her firm little ass into bed. And with the caution, with the split, came the memories.

I first met the Laundry Man in high school. He was just a casual acquaintance then—a friend of a friend, you might say. But I soon discovered that I was more ambitiously horny than I would have ever dreamed possible—and that my three daily hours of football with the high school meatballs didn't alleviate the pain one bit. That knowledge was the birthright of the Laundry Man, and he thrived on it until one day he was bigger than me, and was calling the shots. It soon became my habit to flee the chloroformed vistas of pep rallies and cheerleaders and student body apathy, and to make my way to New York, where I haunted the bars of the Lower

East Side, getting thrown out of most of them for being underage, and the rest for drooling. But I continued undaunted, hunting for that mythical older woman who would, in the privacy of her run-down apartment, teach me every exotic churn and buzzle known to man.

I learned to drink Scotch on the rocks like apple cider, and to perform a number of other routines suggested by fellow travelers—socks in my undertrow, a wedding ring on my finger, a carefully cultivated five-o'clock shadow, and on and on. And I got all the ass I wanted, Grade B ass, to be sure, and not all of it inspected by the Department of Agriculture, but then that's what I was looking for on the Lower East Side. I thought it was all very funky.

But the whole time I was hustling, I was watching. I was comparing notes with the other guys (TWA stewies are best?) and then trying new little numbers out (my wife died of leukemia, she was only twenty) and then watching again. And one day I finally got sick of it, especially sick of the chicks who couldn't play it any other way except as this kind of a game, and more especially sick of myself because I'd been doing it so long that it was part of me, it was there all the time, and I couldn't turn it on and off at will any more. The Laundry Man wouldn't knock off after working hours like the rest of the boys. By the time I stopped going down to New York, I hated the whole riff.

Only to discover that my peers and classmates were now digging the joys of communion. The chicks in school were suddenly hankering for me, mostly because I was aloof. Sweet little homemade lemonade cunts sidling up to you in the corridor and launching into their version of "Getting To Know You." I couldn't stand it. I told them to be quiet, and then to go away, and finally in desperation to fuck off. I became a monk. I avoided them. Because the whole time the Laundry Man was back in my head, stiff with starch and saying, Come on now, son, oblige the lady. Be sociable. Be a man! But I knew better than anyone that the Laundry Man spoke with forked tongue, and I did not want to lie again.

So I tried to keep him under lock and key, and just live my life. But here he was again, huffing and puffing and lusting for the battle—and here was this goddamned chick playing right up to him.

14

She was tapping my shoulder. "Hey," she said, "you planning to finish that all by yourself?"

I looked down at the roach in my hand and laughed. I was about to suggest another, but she already had it out and was lighting it. Then she said, "What do you do in Cambridge?"

"I'm on the dole," I said. It was supposed to be funny, but as I watched her face I could see that she didn't understand. And then, it wasn't all that funny even if you did understand. In fact, it wasn't funny at all. It was a way of life.

"How's that?" she said, head to one side.

"Government," I said. "I study government, political

science, whatever they call it around here."

"Oh," sort of drawing her breath in, trying to figure out if I was leading up to some kind of punch line. I wished there were some kind of punch line for school. "Is that interesting?"

I laughed. "I don't know. Ever read the papers?"

"Only the comics," she said, and I laughed again. That was good.

"Well, there aren't any comics in the government department at Harvard. At least, they don't think of themselves that way. Nothing but serious, devoted scholars."

She said, "Why don't you split? I mean, it doesn't sound like you dig it much."

I shook my head. "Not for a while." Chances were pretty good that if you split, especially if you were splitting to get out of the machine, you'd just wind up a different kind of machine.

"Draft?"

"Uh-huh."

"Can't you get out?" she said.

"Of the all-new, action Army?" I said. "I don't know. What the hell, though, what a drag this is, talking about it like this. This is exactly what they want you to do—get good and freaked-out about something as half-assed as the Army so you can't really concentrate on what's going down. Divide and conquer," I said, raising a mock finger, and she smiled. I finished the joint and put it in the bag with the other roaches. "What're you up to in Berkeley, right now?"

"Working in a studio," she said.

"Is that right?" I said. "Far out. What, modeling?"

She laughed. "No, no. A recording studio." She tossed

her head in the direction of the stereo. "Like, we produced this album, for one, and we do a lot of re-mixing. But pretty soon we're going to be doing the whole works, from beginning to end. They've almost finished the new studio." She pulled out another joint. "Seventy-two tracks, man. Dig that."

"Far out," I said again.

She got up to change the record, and I didn't see but rather felt her presence this time, as she moved about the room in the flickering light.

"Sukie," I said, half to myself, as she sat down again beside me. Rolling it over against the roof of my mouth and seeing it come out with the smoke of the joint, "Sukie." I turned to her and asked, "Why do they call you Sukie?"

She looked up at me and I was filled with her strange eyes, rich and thick, and I couldn't hold the gaze. Suddenly I wanted to kiss her and I folded my hands and thought about Mt. Auburn Street. There, that was better. I could talk again.

"You still haven't told me," looking at her again.

She turned away. "Because I'm, ah, tawdry." She seemed to savor the word as she said it, bitterly, and it dripped from her mouth.

"Tawdry," I said. "Good word. Fine word. Sukie Tawdry. Tawdry Sukie——"

"Don't," she said, and I could hear an edge in her voice, something hurting, and so I didn't. I just sat. And wondered, What now? And wondered again about the Seconal. After a while she put her hand out to me and said, "You're nice."

I was angry. "What?"

"I said, you're nice."

"What does that mean?"—thinking, Christ, Jesus Christ, not this bit, not just now when I was starting to dig you.

"It means," she said, "oh, just that you don't fuck with what you don't understand."

"I'm not nice," I said, withdrawing my hand. "As a matter of fact, I'm impotent. And I don't like people who make jokes about it. So let's have another smoke and forget about it."

She nodded, and as she did she leaned forward to light the joint in the flame of the candle, her skin glowing smoothly, hair pulled back as far as it would go, as if to keep it out of the flame and as I watched her fiercely puffing on the joint, I understood. There was something a little odd about her left eye, which had been covered until now by hair, it seemed a little out of focus. It made me happy and angry at the same time, this ridiculous, dangerous, vicious game we were playing, now that I began to understand the rules, and I could not laugh as I wanted to. Finally I said, "Give me the joint, would you?"

She handed the smoke over and got up to change the record. "What do you want to hear?" she asked, from behind me.

"You just put that on, just a minute ago."

"I don't like it," she said.

"Big deal," I said.

I could hear her flipping through the albums. They made a slapping sound and she said, "It doesn't bother you?"

I was suddenly angry with her for drawing it out. She had trusted me, she had shown me—and now what was all this crap? I said, "Is it supposed to?"

She came back over. "That was not nice," she said.

"It wasn't meant to be."

Very softly, "Are you pissed?"

"No, why should I be?" I was blowing my mind.

She was quiet for a long time before she spoke again. Her voice was full and throaty when she did. "Do you have someone?"

"Are you asking, or do you want to know?" It wasn't exactly what I wanted to talk about, just then.

I flashed on Annie and she said, "Yeah, that happened to me, too."

I looked at her, disbelieving.

"This guy and I had a real good thing going," she went on, "but he thought he could treat me like shit."

I looked at her, feeling something like affection. I thought I was going to laugh when she said, "You remind me a little of him," and I breathed out in a rush.

"Thanks, I'm overwhelmed."

She laughed. "No, no," she said, "just the way he looked. And you don't even look that much like him. He was a prick."

"Oh," I said, not knowing what else to say but suddenly laughing at the whole scene, at the fear and anger which was so important and then not even important enough to be remembered. I looked up at her and she was laughing too.

"The only thing is"—still laughing—"I can't stand those duds you got on. Do you go around like that when you're in Cambridge?" I nodded. "All the time?" I nodded again. "I couldn't stand it," she said. "It must be like walking around inside a tank."

"Yeah, well——"

"Why don't you get out of them?"

"I'm wrecked," I explained, and she just nodded and came around the table and leaned over to undo my shirt. I pulled her down to me on the floor and kissed her hard.

Then she was tickling my ear with her tongue, saying, "Your jacket's going to get dirty."

"It comes clean."

"Come on," she said, "let's get in bed."

"You were taking my shirt off," I said, kissing her. She started unbuttoning and I picked her up and carried her to the bed.

"Is everyone at Harvard such a gentleman?" she whispered, and I dropped her. Laughs.

Somebody was knocking on the door.

"He's not in," I said, and sat down to take my socks off. Another, heavier, knock, and a thick voice asking for me. "Nobody's home," I said. Christ, take a hint.

And then the door was open and three cats were in the room, all wearing gray pin-stripe suits and looking like walk-ons for Robert Stack. Dangling their wallet badges before I could get my glasses on.

"FBI," said the first man.

15

"Your name Harkness?" barked another.

"Yes," I said.

"You rented a '69 Mustang from Hertz today?"

"Sounds familiar. What can I do for you?"

Silence. Then, "We just want to look around." Spoken in typical deadly Oh Nothing plainclothesman tones. Deadly. The speaker was a skinny guy with a crew cut. He had 86-proof brains you could smell across the room, and his neck was covered with acne. He started looking and so did the other two, poking here and there in the room and in the corridor outside.

I suddenly remembered Sukie's lid and got a woozy rush of anticipation, but I couldn't see it on the table, so maybe she'd stashed it. At any rate, I decided to try to get them out of the room as soon as possible.

"Since we haven't been formally introduced . . ." I said. Nobody looked up. "You wouldn't mind telling me what you're doing here?" I continued.

"We would," Crew Cut said. Okay, fair enough.

"In that case, you wouldn't mind producing a search warrant." Fuck these dudes. First thing I'd done when I'd gotten into dealing was to read a manual on search-and-seizure techniques, complete with the latest test cases, rights of the citizen, common police ploys. All the dope, as the saying goes. And so I wasn't about to stand around and watch while these jokers turned the place upside down.

I repeated my question.

"Why don't you shut up," Crew Cut said.

I decided to be indignant. "You know as well as I do that you need a search warrant to go over this place," I said.

Sukie was lying on the bed, the blankets twisted around her, looking unhappily at her dress on the floor. One of the cops stepped on the dress as he walked around the room.

"And I have a witne——"

"Listen, Harkness," the third one said, fat with glasses and a choked, menacing voice, "if I were you I'd keep quiet just now, because——"

"Because what, cop?" I said. I was getting mad. "Right now you're up for breaking and entering, illegal search and, for all I know, seizure, besides——"

"Besides, you're under arrest," Crew Cut said. "For possession. Put your shirt on, you're coming down with us."

I couldn't believe it. I just stared at them as they moved around the room, shuffling and sniffing and poking at things. I was trying to figure out if one of them had picked up Sukie's lid, but they didn't act like it.

"I'm what?"

"Under arrest, candy-ass. Now move it."

If they were bluffing, I figured, I might as well follow them down the line. "On charges of possession?" I said. "I'm clean. Go ahead, look around all you want, you won't find anything on me."

I was scared and Crew Cut was looking pleased. "Sure we don't need a search warrant?" he said.

"Let's go, kid," said another.

There was nothing to do but go. Sukie gave me a So Sad To Be Lonesome look as I got dressed, and I saw how suddenly cold and tired she looked, huddled up in the blanket. Meanwhile the cops kept looking around, but miraculously didn't find anything, not even the roaches. I got all my clothes on and was knotting my tie.

"Forget that," Crew Cut said. "There's plenty of time for that."

I watched them nosing around the room, and felt like laughing. It was almost impossible to take them seriously, with their cops-and-robbers huffing and puffing and the staid, predictable way they played the scene. As if they were actually playing a scene. I felt like I was watching TV—this kind of thing happened to people on TV, not to real flesh-and-blood persons. I was a spectator at my own bust.

Then one of them turned to the dude with the glasses and said, "Hey Murph, you want the girlie?" I felt tight and weak until Glasses said, "Naw. Just candy-ass here."

Then they twirled me around, grabbed both wrists and pulled them tight behind me, and slapped on the cuffs. Wrenched them shut.

"What's the point of that," I said. "I'm non-violent." It was a joke, if a grim one.

"How are we s'posed to know that?" said Crew Cut, dead serious.

"He's bleeding," said Sukie. "You've got them on so

tight he's bleeding." I hadn't noticed, but I took her word for it.

"Relax, lady," said Glasses, the one they called Murph. "Lover-boy here can take it. Right?" He slapped me on the back and I stumbled out of the room.

Out in the hallway I went up against the wall. A good frisk with a knee in the balls, special delivery from Crew Cut.

"What the hell," I said, "you watched me get dressed." Very loud, hoping to wake someone up.

"Shut up," they said, taking me downstairs.

In the downstairs hall, I could see their faces better. Crew Cut was very young, with pimples all over his face as well as his neck. No wonder he was being the tough guy, I thought. This may be his debut. He was glowering ferociously as we left the house.

The second guy looked like a butcher putting on airs. A nouveau riche butcher. Rolled old ladies for their opera tickets so he could fart in a box seat. Butcher needed a shave and some deodorant.

The third guy Murph, the one with the glasses, looked strangely familiar. He was a mean-looking son of a bitch, short and stocky, with closely cropped gray hair, forty-five years old, maybe fifty. His face was smooth, round, complacent: the face of a pig who'd been getting fattened by the farmer all year but hadn't yet figured out what for. His voice was as stiff as his walk and sounded like he'd forgotten how to laugh.

Law and Order, I thought. Bring Us Together.

Outside, the patrol car was waiting, a bored cop in the driver's seat. We drove off into the night, one narc on each side of me. Nobody said anything. The narcs seemed suddenly as bored and passionless as the automaton at the wheel. Finally I said, "What have you got on me, anyway?"

No answer. Everybody was engrossed in the empty, pale night streets.

"Well listen," I said, "long as you're running me in, you might as well——"

"Just shut up, huh, punk?" one of them said. Lazily, enjoying it.

I couldn't believe it. What was this shit, anyway, the drive-ins or a special number they did for guys like me.

After a few minutes one of them turned to me. "We got your friend," he said.

"My friend?"

"Yeah. We got him. Took us a while to find out where you were. Sorry about the delay." Chuckles. I was delighted to see that somebody was having a good time.

"My friend?" I said again.

"Look, buddy, how dumb are you? There's no use fucking around with us. It's over. We got the whole story. Picked up your friend and found the shit. So don't fucking waste our time."

Crew Cut turned around from the front seat to look at me. "See, punk, this time it's for real. It's all for real." Then he laughed. "Christ, you guys are all the same. Like that guy we picked up last week—hey, Murph, you 'member the guy on the beach? Yeah. We picked up this guy on the beach in Frisco last week, busted him while he was shooting up. He had his whole outfit right there with him, along with half a bag of scag, and he was so smacked out of his mind that the whole way in to the station he wouldn't do nothing but tell us what a great guy God was." Titters all around. Crew Cut was being appreciated. "Goddamn. The whole way, the guy stuck to this one story. Said he just went down to the beach to meditate, 'cause he wanted a bag of scag so bad that he'd decided to pray to God, and suddenly—this is what he says, he says, 'and then suddenly, Officer, God answered my prayers, and that bag, my bag you got there, that bag just dropped into my lap, right out of the sky.' Wouldn't tell us anything more. Christ, you guys are all the same."

More titters. Even the cop who was driving joined in. I suddenly felt very uncomfortable.

"I want to see my lawyer," I said.

"Yeah," said Crew Cut. "At the station."

16

I finally got the story when I was booked. Lou was driving around in the car and the brake lights hadn't been working, so the cops pulled him over for a routine check. And Lou hadn't had his license, and nothing but rental papers in place of registration, so they had decided the car was stolen, called in the FBI, and given him a good going-over. Along with the car. It was then that they'd found a lid of Lou's grass under the seat.

So they ran him in, and he swore that it was my grass and my car, and that he'd just innocently borrowed it. He had become extremely helpful, and even gave them Musty's address.

So they busted me.

It was just a freak accident, the kind of dreary, half-assed thing that could happen to anybody. I couldn't even get very angry about it.

The walls of the cell were green.

17

Notes from Jail: Brought to you by the silent majority of Alameda County. Arrival sensations. Jail really exists. Astoundingly dull. In conception, execution, duration, the idea of jail is a watershed in man's inanity to man. Does have its good points. A raving genius couldn't possibly have thought of a simpler way to drive one absolutely crazy. Sense deprivation child's play compared to this. Jail is *will* deprivation. No life. Death meaningless. Ambition a torture. Failure a vision in steel.

More: It goes on. Green everywhere, bathroom green. Like going blind from an overdose of ethyl crème de menthe. County runs a tight ship. Enter jail proper, all personal effects removed and checked. Money, matches, belt, shoestrings. Don't want people hanging themselves by their shoestrings. Then on to converted shower stall, also green, big enough for three men sitting. Five men are standing. Pay phone on wall, am allowed two calls, lawyer and bondsman. Names of bondsmen scrawled all over the wall, no lawyers. Search-and-seizure manual forgot to tell me they take my money away when I come in. I can't call. Others are calling. Suddenly realize they've been through all this before. Have to have been through it to know the ropes, like everything else. Whacked out old bestubbled wino asking everyone if he can blow them. Sorry bud. Gets heavy and I start singing. Very effective. Yell till your lungs burst but singing drives the guards crazy. Transferred immediately to cell by myself.

Cell: Incredible. Everything electric, controlled from out in the hall. No keys, like in the movies. Bars four inches apart and cross-riveted, can't cut and bend. Mine one of eight cells looking onto large room connected to mess room and guards' corridor. Altogether ten doors for the one block, all controlled from corridor. More green. Bare bulbs on all day all night, no sunlight. No air. No idea what time, they have taken my watch. Might slit my wrists. Know that *x* amount of time has elapsed due to unidentifiable slop brought around twice a day. Never eat but go out to mess room, a chance to leave the cell. Doors lock behind even in mess. Four steel slats riveted to wall in my cell, one has a blanket. Somehow it is cold after dinner, good to have a blanket. Light directly overhead through grating, wish I had something to poke it out. Combination can-drinking fountain in my cell, attached to wall. I piss on mess floor. Anything to fuck them up.

Amusements: Good deal of writing on the wall. Jails probably the most creative places in America. No time, have to create your own. Tremendous variety. Slogans, dates, epithets, jokes, obscenities. Some take me back to fourth grade, others brilliant. Everything indelible because scratched into paint of wall. No pens allowed. Layers of painted-over graffiti beneath current coat of paint. Deciphering these provides blessedly time-consuming endeavor. One magazine in cell, old copy of *Life* last seen in parents' living room. The Grandeur That Was Egypt. Very appropriate for jail. All is Lost Empire here. Carefully drawn life-size penis inserted into Nefertiti's mouth on cover. Excellent job. Flash: someone smuggled a pen in to do that. Have to know the ropes.

Not eating makes me sleepy. I sleep a lot, surprisingly good dreams. All of things I cannot have. In one dream I order a Coke, the guard brings it. I wake up crying so happy and see green. Back to sleep. I have no matches and can't smoke. Guards won't give me any, the cunts. First meal third day they come and take me out. Everything sharp and clear in my head from not eating. Gums hurt from no nicotine. Down the hall the desk. This the Out of Stater? Yeah. Two of the plainclothesmen who picked me up are here. No one in cells looks up as I go. Why bother? They're still in. Manila envelope with what looks like my name on desk. Wristwatch, belt, ballpoint, blah blah blah. Piece of paper sign here. Where? Here. Plainclothesmen pull my hands behind again, on with the cuffs. Wait a minute, I hear my voice. First time I've spoken in three days. It sounds crystal clear. Wait a minute, I had twenty bucks on me when I came in here. Frown behind the desk. See the receipt? See your signature? You signed on, you're signed off. So get the hell out. Wait a minute, I repeat, I had twenty bucks, see the twenty in the corner there? Behind the desk heavy now. He'd like to work me over cuffed, I think. So that's your game, huh? he says. Looking at plainclothesmen like Do Him Good For Me. That's your cell number! he says. About face. Have to know the ropes. Forward march past two guards and through a thick steel door, locks inside and out. Small sign on door says BE SURE TO CLOSE TIGHT AS YOU GO. Don't worry, fellas, you don't have to say it twice.

18

Interrogations was a flight up and had padded chairs. It was a small room but on the way up I passed through an office of busy secretaries and big broad glass windows with the sun coming through. And then I realized that if they'd just wanted to interrogate me they could have done it in the cell, and a lot more privately, too. The fact that they were doing it here meant only one thing —I was out.

Inside the room they took the cuffs off and I found myself facing Crew Cut and Fats. They sat and stared at me.

"What day is this?" I said.

"Tuesday," Fats said.

I nodded. Groovy. Economics on Friday. I hoped that Herbie would be in good form when I got back.

Then the third guy came in, the head pig, and sat down at a desk after making a lot of noise taking off his coat and unbuckling his shoulder holster. He reached into his desk and fumbled around for a moment.

I reached into my Manila bag and got out my cigarettes. But no matches. I shook out a cigarette and looked over at the pig, who was still fumbling in the desk. I hoped he was going to produce a light.

Instead he whipped out a plastic Baggie full of grass and stuck it in my face. That was supposed to scare me shitless. I turned to Crew Cut and said, "Got a match?"

"I don't smoke," he said.

I looked at the second guy, who just shook his head slowly, like he could hardly be bothered shaking his head at me.

So I reached into my Manila envelope and pulled out my belt and put it on. Then I put in my shoelaces, and wound my wristwatch, and put my pen in my pocket. Silence until the head pig said, "There are some questions we'd like to ask you."

I turned to face him. "You got a light?"

"I don't smoke," he said. Nicotine stains all over his fingers.

"There are some questions we'd like to ask you," Crew Cut said.

"Before you go," Deskman speaking, significant tone. It was good to know that I'd been right about getting out, and I got a heady adrenalin rush of anticipation. "Tell us about your friend."

"My friend?"

"Now let's not waste each other's time, fella," Crew Cut said. "We've been through all this before."

"We know all about you," Deskman said. I noticed how thick his glasses were.

There was nothing to say. I still wanted a smoke.

"We got your friend, he's in the other room if you want to speak to him," Crew Cut said. Sure you do, chum. "And we've got your marijuana here"—Deskman lifted the bag in the air and gazed at it—"so you might as well play ball. Now are you going to tell us about it or not?"

"About what?"

They didn't blink. "About the whole thing."

"There isn't any whole thing," I said. "I've never been to Berkeley before—I'm a student in Boston and I happen to be on vacation, which is almost over now, thanks to you gentlemen—and I met the girl I was with when you picked me up on Telegraph that afternoon. And we got along, so she offered to put me up." Smirks all around. "And this guy, Lou, whoever he is, needed a car, and she knew him and said he was all right, and I lent him my car. Now the fact that he was busted with an ounce of marijuana in my car may be legal grounds for hassling me, but it doesn't mean I'm going to know what it's all about. I haven't got the slightest idea what he was doing with the dope, or where he got it from. Why don't you ask him?"

"We have. He said it was yours."

"Mine? I don't even smoke marijuana. I haven't touched dope for years. There's a lot of things you can try and pin on me, but a possession rap isn't one of them."

"You've got one on you right now, buddy boy."

"Did you by any chance do any fingerprints off this bag of marijuana? Did you by any chance find any of my prints? Or did you simply take his word for it, that 'cause it was my car it was my bag of dope? Isn't it usually the case that where there's a lid, there's a pound, or a kilo, or a number of kilos? And did you find any dope in the young lady's room that night, or on my person at that time? And have you found any since then?" I was getting worked up and I remembered suddenly the tracks on Lou's arms and decided to take a new tack. "In other words are you doing anything except hassling me on the word of a paranoid speed freak who borrowed my car and then laid a bum rap on me?"

"Relax, Harkness," said Deskman. "Yeah, we did all those things, and we ain't got much on you. But the fact remains that it was your car, and the dope was in it, and we can make things pretty uncomfortable for you on your, ah . . ." he paused, savoring his own thoughts ". . . vacation. Unless you come around and talk dirt with us."

"Talk to you. I have been talking to you. And so far it hasn't gotten me anywhere." I was doing the indignant-citizen number now and enjoying it immensely, after doing time for what even they admitted was a pretty thin hustle. "I want a cigarette. I haven't had one for three days. Don't any of you guys have a match?"

Deskman nodded to Crew Cut, who grudgingly reached in his coat and pulled out some matches. Handed them to me. As if on signal, all three of them pulled out their butts. I lit mine, looked around at all of them, and blew the match out. Threw it on the floor, put the book in my pocket. Crew Cut was staring at me. Deskman again, suddenly, intensely:

"You a good friend of O'Shaugnessy's?"

The question caught me completely by surprise and I was glad I had the cigarette. Took a long drag. It tasted unbelievably good. Meanwhile, my thoughts not at all under control. Had they busted Musty that night, after I'd gone, and were they now keeping it from me? Had they been watching him the whole time, and me, and known why I was in the house? Had they seen my car at the first house that afternoon and followed it, hoping to catch me with something? (It didn't seem like Hertz to have no tail lights.) Had they planted the dope on Lou just so they could run me in? The last made the most sense, 'cause it would explain their letting him off with a few questions, and "taking his word" that it was my dope. Just how much did these pigs know? It was all happening very fast. I decided the least I could do was make them work for it.

"O'Shaugnessy?" I said.

"Yeah, Harkness, you know Padraic J. O'Shaugnessy? Big pusher, long black hair and a moustache? Ring any bells?"

"No, I don't know any O'Shaugnessy. Is this another one of Lou's ideas?" I had to find out.

"No, your friend Lou didn't have anything to do with it. So you don't know any O'Shaugnessy, huh, kid? Fred" —to Crew Cut—"What's the name he uses on the street —what do the creeps call him?"

"Musty," said Crew Cut, with the expression of a man who's blown lunch and missed the bowl.

"Know anybody by the name of Musty?" Deskman asked, leaning forward.

"Musty," I said, trying to sound as if I was mulling it over. "Yeah, I met a cat named Musty. He was with Lou when I met Lou at the house that night. When Lou asked me for the car. Wears his hair in a ponytail, is that the guy you mean?" Said in a tone of intense distrust, as if that were just the kind of weirdo a nice clean-cut Harvard boy like myself could never forget.

"Yeah, that's the one. Seems that you have an excellent memory, Harkness, when you feel like it."

"I do have an excellent memory," I said, "but not for people's last names when I only know their first."

"Okay, wise-ass," said Crew Cut. "Didn't learn nothing in the cooler, huh? That kinda talk's gonna get you nowhere around here. We don't wanna know how smart you are. We know all about you and this O'Shaugnessy. So let's have it. Is he the one who gets you the shit? Where does he get it? Where'd you meet him? Who do you deal the shit to? C'mon, Harkness, let's have it. Now!"

The vibrations in the room were getting a bit tense. They were going through the kind of verbal foreplay that cops do when they're deciding whether or not to really hassle you. But Crew Cut had blown the scene, I could see that from the way Deskman was glaring at him. He'd given it all away. They knew I was connected with Musty, but they didn't know how, or why, or when, or where. And probably they didn't even really know, they just had a damned good hunch.

Deskman shifted position, took his glasses off and looked through them. Put them back on his nose, and said, "Now, Harkness, you got a trial coming up, a hearing tomorrow. You play ball with us and things could go very smoothly. You don't, and your vacation's going to be something of a financial disaster."

Blew it again, Deskman. Trial. Hearing. That meant everything was all right.

"I'm not saying another thing till I see a lawyer," I said.

"You could'a spoke to your lawyer anytime," Crew Cut exploded.

"Not after you thugs took all my money, I couldn't."

"You didn't have any money, Mr. Excellent Memory," Fats said, breaking his silence. "I seen you sign the sheet."

"I had twenty bucks, goddammit, and you saw me tell the guy that, too. And you saw how he hustled me out of it, and you played along with him and dragged me up here. Sign the sheet, my ass."

"You wanna go back down and talk it over with him?"

"I want to get out of here, right now," I said. "I know damn well somebody's paid my bail, or you wouldn't have me up here, and you've got no right to hold me any longer. I'm not saying another thing till I see a lawyer. I don't care if it's just one of your crummy P.D.s. You wanna try and make those phony charges stick, go ahead."

Deskman looked at me, sizing me up. He knew that I knew that it was all over and he had to let me go. But it wasn't over yet. He held the bag up to the light, swung his chair around to face me and shoved it under my nose. "How long you been smoking this shit?" he said.

"I told you, I don't smoke marijuana."

"How long?" he said, like I better answer.

"I smoked, maybe two years. Maybe more. Don't any more."

"O'Shaugnessy turn you onto this shit, huh?"

"No, he didn't," I said. Absurd questions.

"LSD," said Crew Cut, dragging on his cigarette fiercely, "what about that shit, you take that too?"

"I don't recall being busted for that," I said.

Deskman leaned forward, a strange gleam of satisfaction in his eye, as though he'd just destroyed the golden calf single-handed.

"Tell me, Harkness," he said, "is it good kicks?" I looked at him, astonished. So that was the problem. Well, there wasn't anything I could do for his head. I shrugged and said, "Better than alcohol."

It was pointless to bait the pig, but I couldn't help enjoying it when he suddenly began to sweat. His face got red and his lower lip twitched. "Only it's not legal, is it, Harkness? And that doesn't bother you, does it, Harkness? You don't give a fuck for the law. You can't be bothered with what's legal and what isn't. The whole fabric of society is a big joke to you, isn't it? You're just so smart you can do whatever you want, can't you, Harkness?"

"How do you figure that?" I said.

"I don't have to figure it, Harkness," he shouted. "I *know* it. I *know* all *about* you."

"You know all about me?" I said, and looked at him. He was serious. "You should've considered the priesthood, Lieutenant. This isn't a job for you, it's a calling."

His eyes flashed when I said that. He rocked feverishly in his chair for a moment, and then said, "Okay. Okay, Harkness. You're pretty funny, you're a pretty funny guy. You got a lot of quick answers, a lot of smart-guy, know-it-all answers. And you go to your big Ivy League school and wear your English clothes and your old man buys you everything and you're sick, you're sicker than hell and all the bastards like you . . . But let me tell you something, punk."

His face was now very red. I waited for him to tell me something, seeing as how he knew all about me.

"Tomorrow, punk," he said, "tomorrow you're going to be in front of a judge, and that judge is going to know you weren't very helpful. And you're gonna get a felony for all your efforts, see? A big fat felony." He held an open hand out to me, and crushed the air, squeezing the felony, big and fat. "And you might even do some time for this one, Harkness, because society isn't going to put up with your kind of liberal shit any more, you better believe that. We aren't going to put up with it forever—your drugs and your sick life and your disrupting and your crime."

"Disrupting? Listen, I was trying to get some sleep when——"

"Shut up," the pig said. "You better learn to shut up, Harkness, and you better learn fast. Because when you get out of here all your cars and your money and your slick girl friends aren't going to get this off your record, no matter how much you talk. You're going to have to explain this one, Harkness, everywhere you go. Everytime you try to get a job you're going to have to do some explaining, and every time you apply for a loan. And no matter how much explaining you do, it's never gonna go away."

He paused to catch his breath, and shook his head at me. "Sure, Harkness," he said viciously. "I know. Sometimes it happens, a good boy like you. Good family, good education—you just slip up, and make one little mistake. But you've made your mistake this time, see, Harkness, and you're gonna be explaining it for the rest of your life. The rest of your crummy life."

Deskman put out his cigarette in an ashtray next to me, and I could smell the fumes as I said, "Well, it seems that everybody gets their kicks somehow."

19

With that he stood up from behind the desk, and I saw again how small he was. Beware the Small Man. He waved to the other two.

"All right, boys, get him out of here." His face was strained; he was showing great forbearance. I stood up and he came over to me, until he was just a few inches away. I was half a head taller than he was, and he didn't like that.

"You're a really funny guy, Harkness," he said in a low voice. He began to speak slowly, but the words picked up as he went. "A real funny guy, a joker, a know-it-all. I bet all your friends think you're a funny guy and a know-it-all, too."

And with that, suddenly, he kneed me in the groin. It was very quick, and I coughed and bent over, leaning on the desk.

"You're scum," the pig said. "And we're going to break you and your kind of scum, curb you like dogs so that decent people don't have to step in your shit. So decent people don't even have to look at you, see, Harkness? So that they won't even have to know you're there."

And he kicked again, and I coughed again and fell back into my chair, my pack of cigarettes falling out and spreading like white splinters over the floor. The pig gave a final snort and walked out, leaving me doubled-over in the chair, trying to get my breath. When I finally looked up I saw a cigarette being offered. Crew Cut held it out, looking sort of embarrassed to be offering me a smoke, but too embarrassed not to. The other cop was trying not to look at anything, peering out into the outer office.

I took the butt and Crew Cut lit it. After a drag or two I felt a little better. The pain was sliding away. I wiped the tears from the sides of my eyes. "That's a man the force can be proud of," I said.

Crew Cut looked pained, and swallowed a couple of times. "Murphy feels strongly about all this," he said.

"I noticed," I said. "Is he always like that?"

"Murphy feels strongly about these things," Crew Cut said again. "He thought he could find out a lot more from you than he did. He couldn't, so that's that, and——"

And then it hit me. "Murphy?" I said.

Crew Cut and Fats exchanged glances.

"Lieutenant Murphy, old FBI man, now a narc?"

The two of them stood up. It was time to go.

"Didn't he used to work in Boston?" I asked.

"He still does, kid. He's out here following up a smack case. Now let's go."

And I was out the door and through the office very fast. On the way downstairs I began to understand.

20

Lieutenant John L. Murphy was a familiar name in Boston, and a household word in Cambridge. Narc squads are usually distinguished only for their irritatingly obvious presence—you see a freaky guy wearing white socks, and you know he's a narc—but Murphy had been doing his damnedest to change the image. He was tough, fast, and imaginative. He was also a screaming sadist and a crook.

There were a lot of stories about him, but I'd never taken them too seriously. When somebody on the streets tells you about a narc who busts people single-handed, makes deals with them, takes their bread or their dope and then works them over and turns them in anyway—well, that's a little hard to believe. I mean, the image is a bit too desirable to be true. Everybody wants a good reason to hate cops. They're The Enemy.

I was converted when Murphy busted Super Spade. Super Spade was a loping, agile, funky, beautiful, good-time dude, whose face had been glowing in Harvard Square for years, long before the college boys had even heard of dope. Super was sort of the grand old man of the street. Everybody liked him, and everybody was unhappy when he got busted.

After he got out, he came over to see John to borrow some bread for a lawyer. And he blew our minds when he told us the story, because Murphy had busted him and the story was like all the other Murphy stories. Murphy had busted him alone; the warrant was in order, and Super had been caught holding eight bricks. So far so good. Then Murphy began talking about how much Super's eight bricks were worth, and how much time he'd probably draw for that kind of quantity. And Super finally made the connection and suggested that perhaps he and Murphy could work something out.

Which they proceeded to do. Super came up with three hundred bucks in cash and laid it on Murphy. Then Murphy, having already handcuffed him, beat the shit out of him—and then took him in. Next day Super found out he had three charges against him: possession of marijuana, resisting arrest, and attempting to bribe an officer. When he asked the judge how much the bribe had been, the judge told him fifty dollars.

So far it seemed like Murphy was just another rough cop, playing it a rough way. But also in Super's apartment was a glass jar with five hundred acid flats. Super hadn't mentioned them to Murphy, but he found when he got home that the flats were all gone. And soon after that a friend in Roxbury told him about the sudden fast market in the midst of a dry season: all sorts of good acid around, and outasight smoking dope.

Anyway people had been telling these stories for a long time, and it was getting harder to simply dismiss them as street jive. The street people were unanimously in favor of taking Murphy apart, of busting his ass good. Partly because he'd become something of a legend and something of a symbol, but mostly because he had crossed the line and was playing dirty.

A rough and tough cop he could be, and for that he

would be hated and respected. But as a thief with a badge, a guy who broke the rules and regulations we all play by, as that kind of person he could never last.

At least, everyone hoped not.

21

I walked out into the Berkeley sun and stood there, just soaking it up. The light hurt my eyes at first and I sneezed and rubbed my nose.

"Gesundheit," said a voice behind me.

I turned and she was in my arms, crying, kissing me and crying.

"Hi," I said. It was happening very fast, all of it.

"What did they do to you?" she said.

"Nothing. Punched me in the cubes some. That seemed to be about all they knew how to do." I laughed. Getting punched in the chops suddenly seemed absurd.

"Oh, my poor Peter," she crooned, stroking my head.

"Umm," I said, thinking, It was worth it just to feel this.

"My poor, poor Peter," she went on. "You didn't have to do all that."

"What'dya mean?" I laughed. "I didn't think I had much choice in the matter."

"No, for me," she said.

"Oh, Christ, forget it. One bail is better than two any day."

"My poor Peter," she said again, and kissed me.

My rented car was over in the lot. I had the keys back; we went and got into it.

"The hearing is set for tomorrow," she said. "Did they tell you?"

"More or less," I said. I started the car and drove out of the lot, not exactly sure where I was going. I wanted to go to a beach somewhere. A quiet beach.

"Hi," she said, and grinned broadly this time.

We were off.

As I drove I said, "Who paid my bail? Musty?" I would have to wire home for some bread to pay him back. That was good of him. The last time I sat in there until I almost rotted, waiting for somebody to come up with a lousy fifty dollars.

I looked over at her and she was smiling. "What's so funny?"

She just shook her head.

We crossed the Richmond Bridge, and then went through the hills, coming finally to the summit and turning right down an old farm road. The sea was visible from the road but we had to go way down, past miles of grazing land that stood between us and the cliffs down to the water. When we finally got down to the beach, it was deserted.

"Great beach, huh?" I said, but she was already out and running down the sand. It was almost a joyful run, but not exactly. I ran after her and caught her. The sun overhead was fierce and bright.

"Hey," I said. "Who paid my bail?"

She just smiled.

"What'd you do a thing like that for?"

She shrugged. "It seemed like a good thing to do with the money."

"Seriously," I said. I was suddenly in a serious mood. "Why?"

"I don't know."

"Seriously."

"It's a great mystery," she said and giggled, broke free and began walking down the beach. I walked after her.

"Didn't they tell you that they don't give it back?"

"I know," she said.

"Well, why?"

"Don't get frantic." She kicked the water as it slid up the sand. It sparkled off her feet, into the air, then splattered down onto the sand.

"I'm not frantic. I just want to know."

"You're making such a big deal out of it."

"I'm not."

"Yes you are."

And she giggled and started running again, and I chased her, and it all began to seem ridiculous. She was right; I was making a big deal out of it. I finally caught her and tackled her and she laughed very loud beneath me.

"That was a very nice thing you did for me," I said.

She kissed me, pulled me down hard. "You bet your ass," she said.

§

Very stoned, sitting on the beach just back far enough from the water so the sand was dry and still warm from the setting sun, watching the water hiss up toward us. She said, "I can't get me out of your mind."

I knew what she meant.

22

Walking down what seemed like miles of endless corridors, our footsteps echoing, I said, "I'm surprised you have a key."

She laughed.

It was close to midnight, and the building around us was silent. The walls were painted light green, a little like jail; the building reminded me of an institution. "It used to be welfare offices or something," she said, "before it was sold and converted."

"Cheery," I said.

"It gets better."

As we passed them, she showed me the lounges for the performers. They looked like airport lounges or something, sort of plush but impersonal. Very soundproofed. I suddenly began to notice how everything off the corridors was soundproofed.

Then we came into another room, marked STUDIO A. Shock: it was like a heavy living room. Persian carpets on the floor, hangings on the walls, colors and textures. "Like a very nice cathouse," I said.

"Close," she said. And out came another joint. She lit up as I wandered around the room. There were microphones everywhere, and a stand for guitars, and a piano in the corner. I sat down at the piano.

"Do you play?" she asked.

I shook my head.

"You play anything?"

I shook my head, and plunked out "Chopsticks." She laughed, and then said, "Stay there," and left the room. I walked around, breathing in the luxury, and then began to drift into the sense of working with my group, the cigarettes and the quiet talk and everybody getting together, getting their heads and fingers loosened . . .

"Hello," she said. Her voice was funny. I turned around and saw the drapes pulling back to reveal a glass wall, and her behind the glass, staring in at me. The lights in the other room were overhead, harsh and funny. I could see the room was filled with recording equipment, decks and spools and dials and consoles; she was wearing earphones. A flash on the mechanical sense: there was money in all this, and manufactured products, industry just like everywhere else. The flash faded. She made a gesture for me to go toward the microphone.

I tapped it. "Is this thing working?" I heard my own voice, from speakers mounted somewhere in the room. It was working.

"We, uh, just want to play a few numbers that we know well, because we've never played together before."

She knew where that line came from, and she smiled. I began to get into it.

"My name is, uh, Lucifer Harkness . . ."

Something happened. The voice was warbling as it

came back to me. She was flicking buttons. I laughed. "What're you doing to me?"

Now it was echoing, *Doing to me, to me, to me, me.*

"Yeah, well, actually . . ."

This time it was thin, high, squeaky, if your memory served you well. It startled me. "This is getting to be a drag," I said. I wanted to play something, now was the perfect time to be able to do it, but I didn't know how. It was finally hitting home, the foolishness of it, that I couldn't even do simple chords on a guitar, I couldn't do anything. Hopeless. I began to get depressed, and she must have sensed it, because she suddenly came around, opening the studio door, and led me out of there.

"It's because the place is deserted," she said. "Empty buildings are always depressing." She smiled and squeezed my hand.

23

She came to the hearing with me. I had a clean shirt and tie and I stood up straight for the judge. She sat in the back of the hearing room; I glanced back once to look at her.

The judge asked me if my legal rights had been properly attended to, since I didn't have a public defendant by my side. I didn't mention to the judge that I'd been through that whole riff before and it was a drag, because the P.D. doesn't give a screw about what happens to you, he just wants to look good in front of the judge.

So I told the judge that everything had been taken care of, but that in this instance I preferred to defend myself. The judge looked a little amused and a little pleased at that, and told me to proceed.

My defense was pretty weak, but logical. It included such helpful hints as the fact that I was scheduled to leave California the next day, providing I didn't get hung up in jail and cost the good taxpayers additional expense. I also said that I had no relationship with the primary defendant in the case, i.e., the lid of dope, and that I considered it a freak accident that did not merit my bearing the weight of its consequences any more than I already had.

The judge replied that I had a sharp, clever, and discerning mind, but that I obviously knew nothing about the law. Which, he added, meant nothing, since all charges had been dropped by the D.A.'s office, and if I would speak to the clerk before leaving the courtroom, I was free to go.

I was pleasantly dazed. I thanked the judge, who told me not to thank him, and I left.

Sukie laughed as we walked out the door.

24

The next day we went up to Tilden, very early, to watch the sun come up over the Bay. It was cold and dark when we arrived, and we huddled under a blanket drinking Red Mountain and feeling the dry warmth spread outwards. From the top of the ridge you could see everything, Oakland and Berkeley below, and Richmond and Mt. Tamalpais in the distance.

Around six-thirty some freaks showed up and did a dance to greet the morning, while the mists slowly disappeared below and the sun spilled across the Bay. And then suddenly it was time to leave, to return to the world of cars and sewage systems and plane schedules and Burger Kings. We went directly to her room and got in bed, blowing dope and drawing each moment out, as if we could forestall evening.

Late in the afternoon I went downstairs to find Musty, who was in the kitchen, where I'd first seen him. He was drinking jasmine tea, smoking a butt, and selling a couple of bricks to a fantastic-looking thirty-five-year-old chick. The chick split when I showed, taking the bricks with her in an alligator handbag.

"You see?" Musty said, as she left. "All types." Then he grinned. "Look at the ass on her. Beautiful." He sighed, got up, and brought out my ten bricks. "Listen man," he said, "I'm sorry about Lou. He's a little speedy, you know. Bad scene. Does up three bags a day."

"What the hell," I said, feeling magnanimous. "Past tense."

Musty glanced at me as he set the scales on two pounds even and weighed the bricks, one by one. "You're a good head, Harkness," he said. "I can dig why Sukie balls you." I didn't really feel like talking about that. "Got a knife?" he said.

I gave him my Swiss Army job and he sliced the bricks open. They cut clean through, no rocks, no clay, practically no sticks. They were righteous keys, all right.

"Dig the way the blade goes through?" he said. I nodded.

I'd already tasted the dope, so there was nothing left to do but soak the bricks in Coca-Cola for a minute, so they wouldn't smell too bad, and wrap them up. Then into my aluminum-lined suitcase and do up both sets of locks. The ten bricks fit very nicely without shaking or banging when I picked up the suitcase.

Musty held out a hand. "Be cool," he said, "and say hello to John for me."

I went back down the hall, heading for the staircase to say goodbye to Sukie. I dreaded going up those stairs and then down again, but I found her standing in front of the door, raincoat over her shoulder.

"I've got to drop the car at the airport," I said.

She nodded.

"How're you going to——"

"Don't worry about it," she said.

I already had my ticket, so when we got to the airport we just stood around and made each other uncomfortable until they announced boarding for my flight. I kissed her quickly. We were standing underneath a billboard that said GET AWAY FROM IT ALL. I considered taking a later flight and calling John to say I'd gotten stuck in traffic, but the truth was that the East was seeping back into my brain again, the East and Boston and wet roads and hour exams. I knew I had to go.

She kissed me again. "Will I see you . . ." She stopped.

"Sure," I said, squeezing her. "Sure, of course you will." I was definitely getting back into my Eastern frame of mind, I realized, complete with an enormous paranoia about departure scenes and weeping chicks.

"When will I see you?" Very calmly. At least she was calm.

"I don't know. Soon as possible. I don't know."

"I never write letters," she said, not letting up. All I could think was, Why do they always have to do this?

"Neither do I," I said. Which was not completely true. I write them and never mail them. "But I'll call."

"Will you?" Pleased.

"Yeah, soon as my exams are over."

"Tell me what day?" Still pleased.

"I don't know what day. Soon."

"Okay," she said, subdued, and then they were announcing the final boarding call for my flight, and I hustled for the plane.

She said she'd watch my plane from the observation deck, but by the time I was buckled in at the window the sun was almost gone and I couldn't see her at all.

2

Fattening Frogs for King Snakes

It's so sad to be lonesome
And it's too much unconvenient
To be alone . . .

SONNY BOY WILLIAMSON

25

At the airport the crowds of screaming fans were lined up to greet the sensational new rock sensation Lucifer Harkness and his greasy back-up group, The New Administration. Harkness stepped off the plane, resplendent in velvet bellbottoms and a black leather T-shirt; from behind thick purple shades he could see the crowd going wild. They broke through the cordons and fought off the cops and ran screaming for him.

He felt a thousand hands touching him, clutching at his clothes, tearing them off his back, covering him with kisses, biting his neck affectionately, pulling at his balls, and it was delirious and wonderful for several minutes before the cops came down on the kids and broke it up, and Reggie Thorpe, the manager, got the group together and into the waiting Rolls.

As the Rolls pulled away there were hundreds of screaming teenies all lined up on the road out of the airport. Some of them threw themselves in front of the car, stopping it, while others scratched at the glass and kissed it, screaming, "We want to ball Lucifer, we want to ball Lucifer." And Lucifer was thinking to himself about what an unbelievably tedious chore it would be to crack all of those hundreds of green young cherrystones, when the guy sitting next to him jabbed him in the side.

"Hey, lookit dat, buddy. Nice pussy."

I politely looked over a ham-sized forearm to see a thin, wasted-looking chick with a shaved twat lying guilelessly across the centerfold page of *Suburban Jay-bird*.

"Nice," I said. Nice, my ass. The chick was about as ugly as they come, especially without her hair. Hair was mystery, it was sex, it was funky and greasy and it got tangled when you made love.

"How'dja like to fuck her?" he said, holding up another picture.

I shrugged. The woman behind us on the MTA car was doing her best to let us know that she was faint with indignation. She was making small coughing sounds. Out the window, gray and rainy, was the Boston skyline.

"I like 'em with hair," I said. Behind me I heard the sharp intake of breath from the woman.

My companion turned around and shot her a cold look, then turned back to his magazine. "Holy Jeez," he said in a reverential tone. "Lookit, there's one you'd like."

"Yeah," I said. "Now there's a nice bush."

"Christ, you're not shittin'," he said.

He got off at Park Street, leaving me alone with Mrs. Snorts behind me. She got off at Charles Street, the Beacon Hill exit. I took the subway all the way to the end of the line.

26

Shooting out into Harvard Square from the bowels of the MTA was about as much fun as having a tooth pulled without Novocaine. I always felt that way when I got back from the Coast, but somehow I was never prepared for it. Because, as much of a drag as I knew it would be to return, I always figured that it would be nothing more than that—a return. And so the ensuing culture shock, the numbing of mind and body which was only later understood to be Boston's charming way of saying Welcome Back, always caught me by surprise.

And what a surprise. A surprise wrapped in thick, heavy air, dimly opaque light, trimmed with an ineffable, oppressive sense of guilt. The air in the square reeked of guilt. Nobody was ever going to be naive enough to mention it, but it was there just the same, and readily assented to by all on the street.

The street. White pasty bodies and zitty faces shuffled past me, eyes on the ground, clutching cigarettes like drowning men, moving only when the sign commanded them to WALK. Old ladies sneered at passersby and cabbies looked hot and sullen. Three-pieced professors sneaked across the street, clutching their top-heavy wives like illicit Government secrets, and paranoid pristine fags marched poodles past shattered winos bumming dimes. Truck drivers whistled at towny cunts and sad, stooped teaching fellows picked their noses and read the *Daily Flash* in twenty-three languages.

I went across the street to Nini's to get some cigarettes, and cut my way through the prepubescent mob outside. The guys slouched against the walls, sucking on toothpicks or nicotine sticks, scratching their crotches stealthily and yelling at the chicks. The chicks were all over the place, big flowsy broads topped by bleached, ironed hair, chewing the life out of huge wads of gum and swinging their pocketbooks at the more adventurous guys. All the time shrieking like cats in heat, shrieking and laughing and again swinging their pocketbooks. It was too much.

Inside Nini's the adults-only version of the same movie was going on, featuring fat, powdered women, engrossed in multicolored tabloids ("I had a change-of-life baby by another man!"), and the usual mob of skinny, haunted men in the back of the store, tirelessly leafing through the skin mags. Jesus, what all these poor bastards needed was a good lay. And a good lay they'd never get—not in Boston, anyway.

I went down Dunster Street, past Holyoke Center, and over toward the Houses. It was quieter there, and there wasn't any traffic, and the trees had tiny flecks of green at the tips. Spring was getting its foot in the door and it suddenly didn't seem so bad.

Once in the House I stopped to talk to Jerry, who wanted to know all about my vacation. Jerry is the superintendent, a cheerful, sly Irishman who will talk your ear off, given half a chance, and is a stickler for rules, especially those concerning women in the rooms. But Jerry understands those who understand him, and so for a few hours of conversation a term, and a couple of bottles of rye on the Savior's birthday, Jerry is the most amenable and considerate super in the college. Hello, Jerry.

Then up to E entry, and John's room on the first floor. John has a sign on the door which reads:

SEEK AND YE SHALL FIND

John finds this amusing, since his chicks think he means The Truth, while he means the chicks. The door opened to reveal Sandra's lovely form. "How'd it go?" she asked.

I was tempted to ask her the same thing, seeing as how she was decked out in one of John's bathrobes. But all I said was "Fine," and went in and sat down.

John called from the bedroom, "That you, Pete?"

"Yeah."

"Just a minute."

Sandra was looking very chic and wealthily whorish as she put a record on the turntable and sat down across from me. She crossed her legs in the extraordinary way she has of crossing her legs, languidly, with a lazy shot of the bush in the process. Nothing offered, of course, but if she knew you and liked you, she didn't mind letting you know her snatch was all still there.

"How'd it go?" she said again.

"Fine," I said again.

"You look bushed."

"I am," I said.

Then John came out, wearing his other bathrobe. He has two Brooks foulard-print bathrobes. One is several sizes too small for him, and he tells the girls it was a present to him from his grandmother. But it's handy for the girls. John is well-organized about that sort of thing.

"Thanks for meeting me at the airport," I said.

"Hey," he said, "what's this I heard about——"

"A bust?"

John lit a cigarette. "Yeah."

I shrugged. "It happened. I got busted."

"And?"

"They dropped charges," I said. "They couldn't make it stick. It was this other guy's dope in the car and they couldn't make anything stick to me."

John nodded. He didn't seem terribly interested. He pointed to the suitcase. "You get it all?"

"Ten bricks," I said.

"Far out," he said. "Let's have a look." And as I opened the suitcase he said, in a very casual voice, "Was it Murphy who busted you?"

Typical John. The casual fuck with your head. I looked up. "Why?"

"It was Murphy who busted Ernie, you know."

Thanks for the good news. "Yeah," I said. "It was Murphy who busted me and I got off by agreeing to set you up. All you have to do is go down to Central Square tomorrow at ten, carrying these bricks——"

John managed a pretty realistic, hearty laugh. "You getting paranoid?"

"Me?" I said. "Paranoid? Why should I be? My deal's firm." John laughed again, even more convincingly. Then he cut open the brick and I could sit back and relax while he toked up.

The trouble with John is that he had an acid trip last fall and he dropped about two thousand mics with some people he didn't know. The whole thing bent his head around the telephone pole. He never talked about the trip, but from the little he said you could tell he'd gotten very stoned and then very afraid, and decided that the only way he could handle it would be to control it. So he became a controller. Power trips with everyone, crappy little freak games and manipulations and adrenalin spurts passed out at the door, gratis. I had thought he didn't play those games with me, but he did, of course. He played them with everyone.

Which is why John Thayer Hartnup III, of Eliot House and Cohasset, Mass., was into dealing at all. It was the only way it made sense. The son of the Right Reverend Mr. Walker Wingate Hartnup and the former Miss Ellie Winston (of South Carolina) hardly needed the bread. Even if the tobacco money went up in smoke and the Reverend's investments died, Grandmother Wingate could be counted on to call down the First National bankers to her Plymouth home and transfer a few goodies. It was all very far from a question of bread.

Power was something else. A natural talent, it might be called, an inborn skill. He had been an attentive student at Dreyer Country Day, but he was later dismissed from Kent for what the headmaster, without being specific, had implied was a question of drug abuse. It might have had something to do with John's consumption of the Mexican narcotic *Cannabis sativa* during Saturday football games. John had then spoken to the Headmaster in private, and a week later it was announced that John was not being dismissed, but rather had taken a leave of absence because of overwork and stress. No one ever found out what was discussed in the meeting, but John was fond of noting that even such people as Headmasters of distinguished prep schools had soft underbellies.

As a Fine Arts undergraduate at Harvard, a field he had chosen for its casual academic demands and its pretty girls, he had further opportunity to refine his techniques. There was, for example, his nervous breakdown at the end of his sophomore year—a six-week stay at Mass. Mental Health, which brought his parents around to a much more sympathetic stance toward him.

Not perhaps the nicest person, John, but successful in his way.

§

John lit up and inhaled. "Far out," he said. "Count on Musty." And he passed the joint to Sandra, and she passed it to me, and I waved it away.

"What's happening?" he said.

"I've got to work. Hour exam tomorrow."

"Come on," John said. "Get serious."

"Really."

"You're not going to do anything tonight," John said, and he held the joint out to me. I knew it was true, took a hit, and sat back. Stoned again.

Only this time it was jangly and not very pleasant, because I was just back from the Coast, and as soon as I was stoned I felt distinctly rootless, lost somewhere between, and I began to flash on all the times I had felt that way before.

Usually it came from getting stoned with people you didn't know and couldn't get to know, for one reason or another—it was a sudden sensation of being completely alone, but not completely the master of your own ship; the sudden sensation of an immutable gap that separated you from the people you were stoned with. A sense that you were here and they were there; that you were different from them and always would be; that you were locked in yourself and the key was not merely thrown away, but dissolved in organic acid.

A very bothersome feeling.

It was especially bad when it happened with people that you knew, people that you knew too well, in fact. That was horrifying. And I flashed on the time I went home to see my parents.

Well, actually I was ordered down to see them. They threatened a lot of stuff if I didn't come immediately. Because of these rumors they had heard. So about three in the afternoon I got off the train at the Woodfield Station and walked down Elm Street to the drugstore.

I called home after the druggist, a flatulent Rotarian named Mr. Willis, refused to sell me some Vitamin B_{12}. He wouldn't sell it to me because, he said, I needed a prescription, which was a lot of horseshit. I could remember the days when he'd told me I needed a prescription to buy prophylactics. Mr. Willis was the type of solid burgher who felt that the responsibilities vested in him by the community went beyond the purely medicinal. Anyway it was a pain in the ass not to be able to drop a few B_{12}s, because if you're really stoned on heavy dope B_{12} smooths things out a lot. And I was going to need all the smoothing out I could get.

The telephone conversation was short. My mother picked up the phone and said "Hello?" in the sugar-frosted voice that she reserves for those who aren't in the family.

"Hello, mother, this is Peter."

"Oh." Danger, live wires. "Peter, where are you?"

"In Willis's drugstore."

"Where is that?"

"In town, mother."

She got angry then. "In what town, young man?"

"In Woodfield, mother."

"Oh." She paused to consider that one. "Well, you'd better come on out here."

"How?" I said.

"Take a taxi."

"I haven't got any money."

"Oh, you don't?" Very sarcastic. "I thought you'd just be rolling in money, from all your drug deals."

So there it was, out in the open: they had found out I was dealing. What a bummer.

"Yeah, well, mother, I don't."

"Don't what?"

"Have any money."

"Then hitch a ride out," she said. "Your father and I will be waiting."

Click!

Very nice. A very nice and warm person, my mother. I went back outside onto Elm Street and lit up a joint. After three or four hits I felt better, and then I started laughing. Because it occurred to me how ridiculous it was for me to worry about seeing them. They were the ones who were shitting in their pants, just dying to lay into me, nervous as actors before they go on stage. It was their trip, not mine. I already knew by heart what they'd say to me, and once that was over with it didn't much matter what I answered. It didn't matter because my parents didn't have the slightest interest in what I was really up to—in fact, they preferred to remain in the dark. No, the whole point of this scene was to give my parents the opportunity to feel that they were doing their job, fulfilling their obligations to me and to society. In a way they did care what I did; but they cared a hell of a lot more that I knew how they felt about what I did. Groovy. Off to the wars.

I wandered down to the train station and got a taxi, and told the guy my parents would pay him when we got there. Staring out at the Connecticut landscape on the way to the house, I decided I ought to relax a bit. I really wasn't being fair to the parents. I mean, there was no sense in going out there to have a big fight, anybody could do that. I figured that I'd surprise them and be really nice and sympathetic to their trip, and then after things got rolling, and everything was cool, then maybe I could really start talking to them. What the hell, it was worth a try. And I had to be the guy to try, because they sure weren't going to. I laughed when I realized that I was thinking the way a magazine article in *Redbook* would read. Christ, I could see it now. *Noted Young Freak Says: Generation Gap the Kids' Fault!* Rock star Lucifer Harkness bemoans his lack of sympathy and understanding for his parents in his adolescence, and takes all the blame for his rupture with them himself! Amen.

"Which way now, bud?" said the driver.

"Right here, the last house on the left. You can't miss it."

§

"Pay the what?" my father said.

"Taxi," I said.

"What the hell for?"

"He's waiting outside," I said.

"Pay him yourself."

"I don't have any money."

"You never have any money," my father said. "Rich son of poor parents." That's one of his favorite lines. I don't know where he learned it.

"Well, Dad, someone has to pay him."

"You go out and pay him."

"I don't have any money."

We often have conversations like this. Merry-go-round conversations. You go around the circle once, and it doesn't work, so you go around again.

"Well then," he said, "go out and tell him you can't pay him."

"Shit, Dad."

"I might have thought college would teach you more original expression——"

"Shit, Dad. Just pay the guy, will you?"

My father sucked on his pipe and snorted. "Wait here," he said, and went out to pay the taxi driver. When he came back, his face was tight and creased at the corners of his mouth. He was chewing furiously on his pipe. "Your mother," he said, "is very upset. You've made her very upset. So try and be civil when you talk to her, and remember that she loves you very much."

Mother was in the living room, wedged between the two grand pianos. Nobody ever played them, but there they sat, giving the house class. Mother was looking frail and tearful, and it was obvious she had been looking forward to this scene for a while.

"Oh, Peter," she sighed when she saw me.

"Hello, mother."

"Oh, Peter," she sighed again, shaking her head.

"What's the matter, mother?"

"Oh, Peter," she sighed. "Oh, Peter."

My father came in behind. He fixed me with his piercing legal stare, as if I were a walking misbalanced ledger.

"Well now," he said.

"Oh, Peter," she said.

"Do you want your pill, dear?" my father said.

"No, dear," she said, "I already took it."

"What pill?" I said.

"Well now," my father said, turning to me. "Sit down, Peter." I sat down. They sat down. We were all very composed. "You have some explaining to do," he said.

My mother chose that moment to begin crying. "Where did we go wrong, Peter?" she said. My mother cries quietly, no wracking sobs, just tears running down as she stares at you, and she won't wipe them away. It can be very effective.

"Go wrong?" I said.

"Look here, Peter," my father said, relighting his pipe and billowing up smoke screens, "your mother and I have heard some rumors."

"They're not rumors," she said, sniffling, not brushing away the tears.

"All right then," my father said, "let's say we've been told——"

"By who?" I said, jumping right in. I might as well get the story straight.

"Whom," my father said. "That's not important. We've been told——"

"I want to know who," I said. "Mmmmm."

"That's not important. We've been told you are selling marijuana at school. Is that true?"

"Just look at him," my mother said, interrupting. "Look at the way he looks. Don't you have any decent pants, Peter? Those blue jeans with the holes. And your shoes—do you need new shoes?" She looked at her watch. "The barbershops are open until six. We can get——"

"Is it true?" my father asked, fixing me with his legal eye again.

"Yes," I said.

"Oh, Peter," my mother sighed.

"You've upset your mother very much," my father said. He turned to her. "Can I get you a Kleenex, dear?"

"No, dear, I'll be fine. I'm fine." Crying silently.

"You're crying, mother," I pointed out.

"Oh, Peter, Peter . . ."

"I'll get you a Kleenex," my father said, and bolted for the bathroom. He came back with a handful and sat down again. "So it is true," he said, looking back at me.

"Yes," I said.

"Well . . . don't you know it's against the law?"

"Yes."

"Well, doesn't that matter to you?"

"No," I said.

"But it has to matter," my father said. "It's the law."

Now what could I say to that? I'm sorry, it doesn't matter, it just doesn't.

"I don't understand how you can grow up thinking this way, acting this way," my father said.

"It's the school," my mother said. "We should never have sent you away to that school. I knew something like this would happen if we let you go there."

"Now, mother——"

"Well, just look at you, sitting there like something the cat dragged in," she said, letting teardrops spatter on her Villager dress.

"Look," I said, "will everybody stop acting like it's such a big deal?"

"It is a big deal," my father said.

"Dad, look, everybody blows grass at school. Everybody."

"Perhaps everybody that you know, Peter. But I hardly think that——"

"Between ten and twenty million people in this country blow grass."

"I should think," my father said, "that those figures would be very difficult to substantiate."

At this point I sat back. There was no sense in an argument. I used to argue all the time with my parents but it never did any good. One time I'd had an argument with my mother over Vietnam, and she'd questioned some figures I'd used on war spending. "I don't believe those," she said. "Where'd you dig those figures up?" "Bernard Fall, mother." At that, she'd looked irritated. "Well, who in God's name is Bernard Fall?" she'd said. Oh well. I could tell from my father's voice that it was

Perry Mason time again, and I was in the witness box.

"I said," my father said, "that those figures should be damn near impossible to substantiate."

"Look," I said, "do you know anyone who doesn't drink?"

"That's not the issue."

"I'm just asking."

"Yes. I know some people who don't drink."

"But not many," I said.

"We also know some alcoholics," my mother said, "for that matter we know several people——"

"Peter," my father said, interrupting firmly, "there's a difference. Alcohol is legal. Marijuana is not. You can go to jail, Peter. Now, you've lived a sheltered life, all your life. We've tried to see that you were protected against such things. But let me tell you now, Peter. Jail is not pleasant. You wouldn't like it one bit, not one bit."

I sighed. What could I say?

"Now look, Peter. There's nothing we can do about you. There's no way we can stop you or alter your course of action. Looking back, I don't think that there's ever been anything that we could do, as parents. You were always different from the others in the family, always . . . different. But as your parents, we have to tell you when we think you're making a mistake. Can you understand that?"

"Yes," I said.

"We only want what's best for you," my mother said. When she dies, I'm going to have that one engraved on her headstone. The Final Solution to the upper-middle-class children problem.

"Your mother is exactly right," my father said. "That's what I've been trying to say."

I looked down at the coffee table. There was an old issue of *Life,* about the Grandeur That Was Egypt. There was an issue of the *Ladies' Home Terror* on top of it, about Drugs in Our High Schools: A Growing Menace.

"Let's be practical," my father said, shifting around in his chair. "Now I know a little something about marijuana, and I've heard enough to convince me that it isn't the dangerous and addicting drug that everybody says it is. So let's accept that, and go on from there. The fact is, it's still illegal. And it's not a little illegal, it's very illegal. Anyone who sells it runs a grave risk—a risk more serious than any potential benefits that might be gained from the drug itself. Do you follow me?"

"Yes," I said.

"Yes, what?"

That really ripped me. If I hadn't been stoned, I probably would have slugged him in the mouth.

"Yes, *sir.*"

Up until then, up until that fucking *sir,* I had been planning to have a talk with him. I had planned to try, at least to try, to reason with them.

But that *sir* was the end, because it just made me remember what I had known all along in the back of my mind, that all this bullshit about parents and kids reasoning together and overcoming the generation gap is just that—bullshit. My parents wanted to make sure that I understood that their trip was the one that mattered. And at that point I just quit.

All I said was "Yeah, well, look, I don't know who told you all that, but I quit dealing six months ago. I haven't had anything to do with it for six months." This was true.

"Is that true?" my father said. He seemed newly worried about something.

"Yes," I said.

My mother said, "Are you hungry? Did you have lunch yet?" And she wiped victorious eyes.

27

Sandra, sitting next to John on the couch, was wiping the smoke out of her eyes when she noticed her watch. "Oh," she said, jumping up. "It's time. We're gonna miss it." She went over to the television set and turned it on. I was so stoned that I sat there passively and watched her and then the screen, as it glowed to life with the visage of Sally Scott, Eyewitness News, with the Eyewitness News Team investigating a paramount concern to the parents of Boston: teen-age drug abuse.

"Lieutenant Murphy," Sally Scott asked, as she walked along a table laid out, like a feast, with exhibits. "What is this here?"

"This here is a kilogram of marijuana, which is two point two pounds of the drug. It is dried and pressed into a block for purposes of transportation, as you can see."

"I see," Sally Scott said.

"If you bring the camera closer, you might get a better shot," Lieutenant Murphy said helpfully. The camera came closer. "As you can see, this block of the drug is commonly referred to by traffickers and illicit users as a key or a brick."

"And this?" Sally Scott asked, moving on.

"Now, this is what the kids buy from the dope peddlers. This is how the drug is sold, in a one-ounce Baggie. An ounce may cost as much as fifty dollars."

"Fifty dollars!" John said. "Jesus, maybe in Wellesley or someplace."

"I see," Sally Scott said. "And how much of this, uh, drug is necessary to make a person, uh . . ."

"High?" Lieutenant Murphy asked. "Not very much. The drug is smoked in cigarettes, called reefers or joints. Just one of these small cigarettes is enough to make a person suffer all the effects of the marijuana plant."

"Suffer?" Sandra asked, genuinely puzzled.

John grinned.

Sally Scott said, "And what exactly are these effects?"

"Mostly unpleasant," Lieutenant Murphy said. "The mouth feels dry and the voice may be painful. The eyes hurt and one may suffer hallucinations. All inhibitions are released and the person under the drug may act in peculiar and bizarre ways."

"In what ways?" Sally Scott had unusually large eyes.

"Someone on this drug, under its effects, stoned, as the psychologically addicted users say, such a person is capable of almost anything."

"I certainly am," Sandra said, and got up and switched the television off.

"Hey," John said, turning it back on. "Roll a joint, Sandy." The sound returned just in time to hear Sally Scott ask ". . . the magnitude of the drug problem in Boston?"

"Very serious," Murphy said seriously. "There's no question of that. All reports indicate that the center of drug abuse in the country is shifting from San Francisco to New York and Boston. Boston is now the center."

"Why is that?" Sally Scott asked.

"The climate," said John.

"Primarily because of the influx of college students to the Greater Boston area. We have two hundred thousand college students, most of them from out of state. Unfortunately, some of these students deal in drugs." Murphy paused to get his breath, then went on. "You see, the atmosphere on the college campuses today tends to encourage bizarre behavior, and often the responsible adult on the scene, the administrator, and so forth, will pooh-pooh even illicit activities if they happen to be fashionable. The campuses also provide a gathering place for all types of weirdos, outcasts, and hangers-on who wouldn't be able to exist in a normal American environment. These types are often among the offenders. Simply by their presence, they assist the growing drug traffic."

"Oh, Christ," John said, "are you listening to this bullshit?"

Murphy was gone, and Sally Scott was saying: ". . . University's psychopharmacology unit for answers to these and other questions. Doctor, what is the medical evidence on marijuana?"

The doctor was pale and thin and thoughtful-looking. He wore glasses and blinked his eyes a lot, and spoke in little shotgun-bursts. "Well the first thing to say—is that there is very little in the way of—hard medical data on the drug. On the contrary we know remarkably little—about the effects—or the hazards—of this particular compound; however—we can say—that earlier ideas were wrong—and the drug is not addicting—by this we mean—there is no tolerance—phenomenon—and no psychological dependence or physical—uh, dependence—craving—no craving—and we can say the drug does not lead—to heroin or other narcotics."

"You say heroin or other narcotics. Isn't marijuana a narcotic?"

"Well, that depends—on your definition—but strictly speaking, a narcotic means—something that produces sleep—from *narcos* in Greek, 'to sleep'—but in the usual sense it means pain-killing and sensory-dulling medications—sleeping pills—and these drugs, as you know, are nearly all addicting—the term narcotic—to most people—means addicting drug—though not, of course—to doctors." Blink, blink.

Sally Scott looked him right in the eye. "How dangerous is marijuana?"

"Well, that depends again—on your definition—an automobile—is pretty dangerous—and so is aspirin, liquor, and cigarettes—the same thing—all medications—all drugs, broadly speaking—are dangerous and you are better off without them. In terms—of purely pleasure-producing drugs—like cigarettes and coffee—and alcohol—we can say that marijuana—so far as we know—may be a better drug to take—for pleasure—that is, safer and less addicting—but then—we know little about it."

"When you say a better drug . . ."

"In terms of side effects—long-term damage—something like alcohol, as you know—is a terrible drug—physically addicting—psychologically disrupting—literally a poison to brain cells, a neurotoxin—and yet it is perfectly acceptable—to society."

"Alcohol is a poison to brain cells?" Sally Scott asked, astonished. "But alcohol is used in all civilizations around the world."

"Yes," the doctor said. "That is true."

After half an hour of this, I got up off the couch and said to John: "Got a lid?"

John raised an eyebrow. "Studying?"

"The exam's tomorrow," I said, "and I don't know a fucking thing about the course."

John shrugged.

"Well, it's not Spots and Dots, you know," I said. Spots and Dots was the toughest course offered by the Fine Arts Department. Modern Western Art 1880–1960. Blind men had been known to pass.

"Top drawer of my dresser," John said. "But only take one."

"Yeah, yeah, yeah," I said. I opened the drawer and took a Baggie, one of the fuller-looking ones. Herbie was particular about his payoffs. When I came back, John said, "By the way, check your desk?"

I shook my head, and went into the other room to check my desk. There was a stack of mail on it; on top, in a cream-colored envelope, some sort of invitation. The handwriting on the front was Annie's. I tore it open.

It was an invitation to attend the Piggy Club Garden Party the next Saturday. I looked at the postmark on the envelope; it had been mailed a week before. Too late to give a negative reply. I went out and threw it in John's lap. "Did you rig this?"

John looked shocked. "You mean, arrange it?"

"No, dammit, I mean call her up and tell her I was out of town."

John said, "I knew you'd be back in time." He smiled. "To accept," he added.

"Get bent," I said.

"It's a peace offering, you know," John went on. "It means she still likes you."

"Get bent," I said again. John was a member of the Piggy Club, and he was having a moment of fun at my expense. We both knew that Annie was now making it with a club member, and we both knew that club members were not permitted themselves to invite women to the parties.

"You don't want to go?" John said, now acting surprised.

"Me? Not want to go to the Piggy Club Picnic? You've got to be kidding. I can hardly wait."

"Garden Party," John amended. He sighed. "Little late to call her up and refuse, isn't it?"

That was unnecessary, and as I left the room I slammed the door behind me. Typical John interaction. I was furious and, in a sense, grateful for the pressures of the coming exam. No chance to brood on it. It feels so good when I stop.

Down the hall was Herbie's room. Herbie was a weird little cat, sort of a cross between Mr. Natural and Dr.

Zharkov. He was a senior, and seventeen years old. He'd come from somewhere in West Virginia, where his father worked in the mines and his mother worked in the mine offices; one of those trips. Mother had noticed very early that Herbie was not like the other children and had taken him to a testing center that the government ran for mentally retarded children. The testing people had found that Herbie's I.Q. could not be accurately measured—and not because he was retarded. They'd sent him to a special high school in New York, and then they'd gotten Harvard interested in him. Herbie hadn't taken a math course that was listed in the catalog since his first year at Harvard, nor, for that matter, an economics course or a physics course. He was now working up at the Observatory, taking a side degree in astrophysics.

I came in and found him sitting in his bentwood rocker, rocking back and forth. He wore dungarees and a garish print shirt, and he was smoking a joint the size of an expensive cigar.

"Peter," he said, when he saw me.

"Herbie," I said, and sat down across from him.

Herbie scratched his head. "Let's see, now." He looked across the room at a wall calendar. "Economics, is it?"

I nodded.

"All right," he said. "We can take an hour." He held out his hand. I dropped the Baggie into it. He squeezed it, feeling the texture, then held it up to the light; finally tossed it onto his desk. "Sold," he said. "There's paper and pencil on the desk. Let's get started. It's all very simple," he said. "The internal dynamics of the European nation-state in the early part of the seventeenth century eventually necessitated the manipulation of the economy to serve the political interests of the state. That concept in turn led—am I going too fast?"

"Just fine," I said, scribbling as fast as I could. "Just fine."

28

I hate the mornings before exams. I always go to breakfast, because I've been up all night, and I feel really ragged, and I have coffee and that makes me feel even more ragged. And I read the paper and shoot the shit and try to forget that I have an exam at 9:07 and that I haven't studied for it.

If you can get with some good breakfast discussion, then you can forget the exam coming. A discussion like whether women with small boobs have better orgasms than women with big boobs.

But there wasn't any such discussion the morning after I got back from San Francisco. I just sat there with my coffee and notes, and I felt ragged. It was so absurd, the school riff: all that time spent in school, which in the end amounts to the morning of an exam and the hour or two of the exam itself.

Across the dining hall, a few industrious wimps were still studying: jamming down those last few pages of notes, knowing full well that it might make the difference between an A-minus and a B-plus. I thought of the Romans stuffing themselves with food, then sticking their fingers down their throats, vomiting it up and starting to eat again. Of course, if you eat that way, you must be much more interested in the process of eating than you are in the nutritional value of the food you take in. You must also have the stomach for it.

Pretty soon the wimps were dumping their trays, and hustling feverishly out the door, talking to themselves. The time had come. I got up and left with them.

§

The exam was held in Memorial Hall, a cavernous medieval sort of building, with desks in long rows. The proctors wandered from desk to desk with their hands clasped behind their backs. The best proctors—the most professional ones—remained entirely and haughtily aloof. But the graduate students and section men who were there to answer questions about the exam questions, as well as to be proctors, were pretty bad. A lot of them liked to walk from student to student and check out what was being written.

About halfway through the hour one of them stopped to look over my shoulder. He looked, and he stayed. I kept writing, getting suddenly nervous. He had a nose cold, this proctor, and he sounded like a horse with pneumonia on a cold winter morning. Finally I turned back to look at him.

He was shaking his head as he read the page.

I shrugged.

He shrugged back, but at least he walked on. The bastard had shaken me up; I began having trouble concentrating on the question. Particularly since I hadn't done any of the reading that was necessary to answer it.

I was just sort of going along, putting down words. The answer didn't mean anything, but then neither did the question.

I began to think of Sukie, and how she had looked when I left her at the airport. I wondered if she made it back all right. It was a drag for a single chick to hitch out to Berkeley at night. And then I wondered if she was meeting somebody afterward. I wondered if she had just wanted a ride to S.F., and that was why she had come in.

Then I started to think about how she had been in bed. It was obvious that she wasn't learning anything from me, which was completely to be expected, but just then it seemed outrageous, absurd, that she should have been with anyone but me. Or that she ever would be with anyone but me in the future. I could feel irritation building, and I realized that I was jealous. Not even jealous, more . . .

"Five minutes," the king proctor said, stepping to the microphone.

I looked back down at my bluebook. I still had another essay to go. I stared at the question, praying for inspiration, and I got it at the last minute.

29

I have never been jealous. At least, not about women. I have been jealous of objects, of things, and sometimes of traits; I remember especially a friend of mine when

I was a kid. He held my unbroken admiration for years, because of his imagination. He effortlessly devised such wonders as the Burning-Bag-of-Shit Trick, conveniently placed on a neighbor's doorstep—when the neighbor tried to stamp it out, well, that was his problem.

Also the Good Humor Man Stunt, in which one kid would sprawl out on the road, deathly ill, and enlist the Good Humor Man's help, while another kid went to the back of the truck and climbed into the refrigerated compartment. There he would stay, eating himself sick, for a full block, at which time a similar catastrophic mid-road illness would again cause the truck to stop, and allow the half-frozen and satiated ice-cream fiend to escape giggling and shivering into the sunlight.

And I remember I was jealous of a guy who lived down the street from me one summer who had a cycle before I even had a driver's license.

But as far as chicks went, I had never really felt anything. Certainly not jealousy. Chicks had been a necessary evil, giggling half-wits who played games until your balls were purple and then forgot their purses in the theater, or had to be in by midnight, or Weren't That Kind of Girl, or some other crap.

And yet there I was, finished with the exam and by all reasonable expectations hot on the trail home, to blow some dope and collapse into bed, after being up almost forty-eight hours. But that wasn't happening. Instead I went right back to my room and called her.

The phone rang a long time. Finally a dull voice said, "Hello?"

"Hello, is Sukie there?"

"Who?" A very dull voice, and then I remembered the time change.

"Sukie Blake, Susan, is she there?"

"What number are you calling?" the guy said. He was being very, very careful about waking up and I couldn't stand it.

"Sukie, man, Sukie, the blond chick who lives upstairs, the one with the weird eye?"

"Oh." He mulled that one over. "Yeah. Hold on."

Then there was a silence. I stared around my room and lit a cigarette and blinked in the smoke.

"Hello?" Dazed voice.

"Hello, Sukie?"

"Who is this?" Really dazed.

"Sukie, what's going on out there?"

"What?" She was beginning to wake up. "Who is this?"

I thought I heard some sound in the background. Some sound in the room. "Are you alone?"

"Goddamn it," she said. "Who is this?"

"Peter," I said.

She laughed. Three thousand miles away, I heard that laugh, and it made me smile. "Oh, Peter," she said. "It's seven-thirty in the morning."

"I'm sorry," I said. "I wanted to talk to you."

There was a yawn at the other end, then, "How was your exam?"

That made me happy. She'd remembered I was going back to take an exam.

"Terrible. I thought about you the whole time."

"What kind of an exam was it?"

"Economics."

"Peter, that's not good, you thought about me during an economics exam?" And after another yawn: "What did you think?"

Hmm, what did I think? That was a drag over the telephone. "Oh, you know."

There was a pause. A short pause while she woke up still more. "You wanted to know if I was alone," she said, her voice low and amused.

"No," I said, "you weren't awake. I asked how you were."

"I'm not alone, Peter," she said. "When you called I was in bed with eight puppies."

"I didn't ask you whether you were alone," I said.

She gave a low laugh. "Peter, you're sweet, do you know that?"

Well, that was it. Like walking out on a limb, and finally the limb snaps. I looked around the room, the goddamned dreary room, and I said, "Listen, I want to see you."

She laughed again. "I want to see you, too."

And then in a sudden rush I said, "Then why don't you come out here?"

"To Cambridge?"

"Sure."

"How, Peter?"

"I don't know. There must be some way."

She asked me then if I had any money. I didn't. I asked her. She didn't. Swell.

"Swell," I said.

It was quiet on the line. A kind of depressing quiet.

"Maybe," I said, "I can figure out some way to come

out there." But I knew it wasn't true. In a few weeks I would have to start studying for finals. She must have known it wasn't true, too, because she sounded sleepy again when she said, "All right, Pete."

"No, really. I'll figure something out."

"I know. I believe you."

And I guess in a way she did. Finally she said she was costing me money, and I said the hell with the money, but I couldn't really afford to say that, so I hung up and realized that I was very tired and that I wanted to sleep for a long time.

30

I didn't wake up until lunchtime the next day. I am a man of few vices, one of them most unquestionably being the time I spend with my eyes closed. But as soon as I was up I was remembering Sukie, and the phone call, and all she'd said.

I caught up with John in the dining hall, and joined him over a plate of sawdust and beans.

John looked up and smiled. "Peter," he said. "How's the head today?"

"Fine. How're the eats?"

"Awful," said John. "I didn't expect to see you for quite a while. Heard you had a little trouble with that economics exam yesterday."

"Trouble?" I tried to look surprised.

"Heard you barely finished."

I sighed. I thought he'd been talking about the Senior Tutor. I get messages from the Senior Tutor three times a year: after fall-term hour exams, after mid-terms, and after spring-term hour exams. I was expecting one any day now, but at least it hadn't arrived yet.

"No, that was no trouble," I said. "Just had better things to think about."

John laughed, and then frowned at his potatoes. "Jesus," he said, "what the hell is that?" He held a clump aloft for all to admire.

Somebody said, "A hairpin."

"A hairpin, Jesus," John said. "I could get lockjaw or something from eating this crap. Look at it, it's rusty."

I'd had enough to eat right then. "Heard from Musty?" I asked.

John looked up sharply. "Any reason why I should've?"

I had to play this one right. I didn't want to keep anything from John but then again I didn't want him to fuck me up, which he undoubtedly would if he had time to do so. All I said was, "No. Nothing special."

John dropped his potatoes and lit up a smoke. "Okay," he said, "what's the big secret?"

"No secret."

"Well, then, what's all this garbage about Musty? C'mon, Peter, I've known you too long to just think you're wondering out loud when you drop something like that."

"Like what? Christ, you're as paranoid as all these other creeps." I spread an arm out to encompass the dining hall, which was filled with guys studying over their meals. "You've just got a different angle on the paranoia, that's all."

"Uh-huh." John nodded grimly. He blew some smoke in my direction. "Then who were you calling after the exam yesterday? Not Musty, by any chance?"

I had to laugh. John managed to have a finger on anything that went down.

"No, not Musty. I was talking to a chick."

John put his smoke out and laughed heavily. "A chick, eh? Not a California honey, by any chance? Yes?" He sat back and sipped at his coffee. "Far out," he said, "far fucking out."

"What's far out?"

"Nothing. It just makes sense, why you've been blowing your mind ever since you got back here two days ago. And me thinking it was the climate." He laughed again. "Far fucking out." He looked suddenly serious and leaned over to me, across the table. "What'd she tell you about Musty?"

"I told you already. Nothing."

"Then what's this riff all about?"

"I was just wondering if you had any more trips lined up, in the near future."

"California trips?"

"No, mescaline trips."

"What's wrong with you, you got blue balls after a couple of days around this lady?"

"You might say that. You might just say I want to see her. What difference does that make? You got any trips lined up, or don't you?"

John searched his coat for another butt. "Not in the near future. Not till after exams, I'd say." He cocked his head and said, "But even if I had a run lined up, you wouldn't be able to do it . . ." letting the statement wander off into a question. I knew what he was asking.

"Aw, hell," I said, "I could probably work something out."

John took a long drag on his smoke and nodded. "That's good," he said. "That's good to hear you say that, Pete, 'cause I wouldn't want you going around with some kind of wild misconception in your head about me letting a chick run the dope in."

I searched around for another smoke and thought that one over. I'd known he would say that—John never let chicks in on his deals. It was a completely bullshit prejudice, because chicks were cooler for a run, if anything, than a long-haired dude could ever be. Most big dealers on the Coast, in fact, used only chicks—but I wasn't on the Coast and I wasn't talking to a Coast dealer. I was talking to John.

"Supposing," I began, "supposing you couldn't get anyone around here to do the run? Would you consider letting her do it then?"

John looked pained. "Peter," he said, "you don't seem to understand. You know how I feel but you don't seem to understand. Well, I'll tell it to you all over again." He paused and then said, very deliberately and carefully, "Chicks . . . fuck . . . up." He looked at me.

"I was just wondering."

"Well, you can stop wondering."

"Even if you couldn't get anyone around here, and you had a run set up and a courier was all you needed, you wouldn't let her do it?"

John was quiet when he said, "Never. Never, never, never. I'd change the run, I'd can the run—Christ, I'd even do it myself. But I'd never count on a chick to get anything through. Chicks fuck up."

I shrugged, and stood up. There wasn't anything else to say. I knew that if Musty called in a few days and told John that he only had a day or two to get somebody out to San Francisco to make a quick run before he split for Oregon, John would bust his ass to get somebody. What I'd been hoping was that John would at least admit the possibility of letting Sukie be that somebody. But he wouldn't, so I had to get to her. There was no other way.

31

I needed a hundred and sixty bucks to get to the Coast on a plane. I wouldn't have needed anything to hitch, but I didn't have the time for that. So it was all or nothing, and after a few minutes in front of the Student Union Jobs board I began to think it was going to be nothing. I could get two-fifty an hour translating Sanskrit into German for Professor Popcock, which wasn't exactly my field, or I could get two-eighty bartending on weekends. But I'd already turned down a few of the bartending boys' jobs in order to make the run, and they took an exceedingly dim view of those who didn't exercise the right to work when it was waved in their faces. I could go in there bleeding right now, on my knees, begging for a gig, and they'd tell me to beat it.

That left a kitchen job as the only real alternative, at one-eighty an hour, which would be two fifty-hour weeks, and I was just about to run down and sign up when I noticed a little note saying that students couldn't work more than twenty hours a week. Far out, that was about all I had to say.

I went out into the courtyard to take a walk and think.

Once outside, I met Herbie, who was going to the library. I walked along with him, and asked him how I could make a lot of money in a short time. He said, "Eye Tee Gee."

"What?"

"Get yourself twenty shares of ITG. In six weeks, you'll be rich."

"What?"

"ITG," he said patiently. He had learned, in his seventeen years, to be patient. "Over the counter. It's really taking off."

"How much is twenty shares?"

"Two hundred dollars," Herbie said.

I said I didn't have it.

And Herbie, to my dismay, said he didn't know any other way.

"Are you sure?"

Herbie sighed. "Peter," he said, "you're talking about legal bread, right?"

"Yeah. Legal bread."

"Well, that's a problem, making money fast and legally," Herbie said, as if it was something I really should have learned a long time ago.

32

I wandered around the next two days, looking for jobs and asking people what they knew, but nothing turned up. I was just starting to think that hitchhiking wasn't such a bad idea when I got the note from the Senior Tutor. That was the end. I knew what he'd want. He'd want to tell me that I'd screwed the economics exam—probably royally—and that if I continued to screw things he wasn't going to be able to help me very much, except to plead my case before the Ad Board and try to keep them from booting me out. Which was cool, his concern and all, but that wasn't really what went down at a meeting with the Senior Tutor. Those meetings consisted mainly of him telling you how much he worried about you and your work and your habits, which was a drag, and they always ended with him asking you a lot of nosy questions he didn't really want the answers to, but somehow felt compelled to ask. His field was the minor poets of the eighteenth century, that was the kind of dude he was. Well, the hell with it. I had to go and see him.

He met me at the door of his study, and escorted me to a padded chair with an arm under my elbow.

"Well, Harkness."

"Sir."

"Well, sit down."

"Thank you, sir." I sat down. As I did he turned away

from me, to look out the window. All I could see of him were his hands, which twisted and turned as he built up steam for our little chat. Finally he turned again to face me.

"Harkness, you probably know why I've called you in today."

"Sir."

"I said, you probably know why I've called you in."

"Yes, sir. I have a fairly good idea."

"A fairly good idea. Ah-ha." He went over to his desk and began to fill his pipe. The Senior Tutor had a way of repeating things that you'd said as if they were meant to be funny. It was not very amusing.

"And what would that fairly good idea be, may I ask?"

"I suppose that I screwed that economics exam yesterday."

"You suppose that you—ah-ha, yes. You mean to say that you suppose that you did poorly on the exam."

"Yes, sir."

"You did poorly, Harkness, you did very poorly." Pausing to light his pipe. "You flunked it, as a matter of fact."

"Sir."

"I said you flunked it."

"Yes, sir."

"Well," he said, looking up from behind billows of smoke. "Is that all you have to say?"

"What else is there to say?" I said. "What's done is done."

He smiled benevolently at that. It was one of his favorite sayings. "Well, yes," he said. "Now I assume that you know what your failure means?"

"I think so," I said.

"It means that your period of academic probation will not end this spring, but will continue next fall. Until the end of the fall term," he explained.

"Yes, sir," I said.

Having finished with that, the Tutor seemed suddenly relieved. He sat down in front of me on the edge of his desk, as if to show me how he was letting his hair down. Business was done, and now it was time for an intimate chat.

"Now, Harkness," he said. "I've been looking through your folder. While I've been waiting for you, you see, just glancing through. But I must say that I don't understand your case at all. Not at all."

"Sir?"

"I've been looking at your high school records, both scholastic and athletic. And your recommendations. And the comments of your freshman proctor and advisers, that sort of thing."

"Sir."

"And I don't understand it at all. You're not performing up to expectations, Harkness. You know that, of course."

"Yes, sir."

"Yes. Well, I was wondering if you could give me any clues as to *why*. From all the indications of your record, you should have been a sort of Harvard Frank Merriwell."

"Thank you, sir." Bloated ass-hole.

"I've been wondering if there are any problems you might be having. Personal problems, family problems, financial problems? That I might assist you in straightening out?" He looked at me, but I tried to look blank. "After all," he said expansively, "that's what I'm here for."

"No, sir," I said. "I don't think there are. But thank you anyway." Nosy bastard.

"Well, Harkness," he went on, "I was wondering, because I've noticed a certain trend in your behavioral development, if I may say so. For example, you came here all All-American in football, and yet you quit after the first half of the season."

"Well, sir," I said, "if you knew the coach, I think——"

"Now, now," he said, holding up his pipe, "just let me finish. You quit playing football, and shortly after that your grades dropped. The next year, last year that is, you were involved in one of the radical student political organizations that we tolerate here on campus. And you achieved some prominence in that endeavor. But you quit that too. Now, during this year, you haven't pursued any organized activities that I know of, so you haven't quit anything. But it doesn't seem to me that you've been *doing* anything, either, Harkness, if you will permit me to say so."

"Sir," I said. Nothing more. The imbecile.

"Well," he said, "do you have anything to say?"

"In my defense, sir?" I cocked my head.

"Oh, come now, Harkness," he said, getting off his desk, "that's distorting my meaning quite deliberately, don't you think? I'm not trying to accuse you of anything, I'm trying to help you."

"Thank you, sir. But I don't think I need anyone's help right now but my own."

"As you wish," he said.

"Thank you, sir," again.

"Well," he said, "hope you do better next round. And if anything comes up, don't hesitate to come and see me. My secretary will make an appointment for you." Edging me to the door.

"Thank you, sir," again.

"It's normally a week or so from the appointment to the meeting, but if you feel that you have something important to discuss, we could make it a day or two, you know."

"Thank you, sir," again.

He opened the door, looked out at his secretary and the crowded sitting room, and then closed it.

"There is just one more thing I should like to say to you, Harkness. As regards your record."

"Sir." Here we go again. The old fart could never find a last word that really suited him, so he just dribbled on endlessly.

"Sit down, Harkness, sit down." He filled his pipe and snuggled into his chair. "It's not exactly my field," he began, "but I've made a quite extensive study of the man and his work. And I think that, in some ways, my conclusions about him can be applied to you, as well."

"Sir?" I said. What was this routine?

"De Quincey," he said, "Thomas De Quincey. Are you familiar with his work?" Puffing on his pipe fatuously.

"Only vaguely," I said, thinking, Of course I am, moron.

"Yes," he went on, as though he would've been disappointed if I'd said anything else. "A very interesting fellow, De Quincey was." He paused and looked at me. "*Is*, I should say, in light of your case."

"Sir?"

"Are you, ah, at home with his little volume on the aspects and vagaries of the opium-eater's existence?"

"No, sir." God, not this.

"Well, De Quincey was an addict himself, you know, an opium addict. And he wrote a fascinating little study of his addiction, entitled *Confessions of an English Opium-Eater*. Fascinating." He glanced over at me to make sure that I was with him, and I nodded. "And in the course of his account, he makes some extraordinary observations." Looking at me again. "For instance, at one point, he remarks that 'opium eaters never finish anything.' That's a wonderfully, oh, to-the-point remark, don't you think, Harkness?"

"Telling it like it is," I murmured.

"I beg your pardon?"

"Yes, sir, it is."

"Yes," he said, "I quite agree. Well, do you see the connection, then, do you see what I'm driving at?"

"Yes, sir," I said. "I think I do."

"Uh-huh," fumbling with his pipe, which had as usual gone out. "And do you have any, ah, comment on the matter? Does it strike a responsive chord, I should say."

"I don't believe so," I said.

"None at all?" he queried. Man, he was begging for it.

"Only an intellectual one," I said finally.

"Ah-ha," he nodded. "And what is that?"

"Artaud," I said. "You're familiar with Artaud, I take it?"

The Senior Tutor blinked. "Well, he's not in my field, you understand, but yes, I think that I'm familiar with the rudiments of the man's work." That got his goat, the old turd. I was playing it his way, and it hurt.

"Artaud was also an addict, an opium addict, that is, and his comment on the matter was that . . ." I paused, trying to get it out right ". . . his comment was that as long as we haven't been able to abolish a single cause of human desperation, we do not have the right to try to suppress the means by which man tries to clean himself of desperation." I paused and looked at the Tutor. "Those were his words on the subject. Of course, Artaud was himself a desperate man when he wrote them, desperate in a sense probably unknown to De Quincey. Because when he wrote his little essay on opium they were getting ready to cart him off to the madhouse. And not for being an addict," I added.

"I see," said the Tutor, who looked as if he didn't know what the hell I was talking about. "Yes, I see. Artaud. I'll have to look into him. He was one of those Cruelty fellows, wasn't he?"

I nodded.

"Yes. Well." He stood up again and held out his hand. "It's been good talking to you, Harkness, and remember, if you should think of anything that you want to discuss, or perhaps if you should just feel like a chat, don't hesitate to let Miss Burns know."

"I will," I said, "and thank you, sir."

"Yes, yes," he said, showing me to the door.

33

Two days of earnestly anemic study went by and then John marched into my room and plunked down on the bed.

"How's it going?" he said, which I did not bother to respond to because John didn't give a goddamn how it was going and never had. All he meant was that he had something on his mind. He pulled out a joint. "Want to blow some?"

I shook my head. I was feeling virtuously studious, and I knew that the dope would kill that. I also knew that I couldn't sit around and watch him smoke too long, so I said, "What's happening?"

"Well," John said, "I'm thinking about this Lotus, it's in beautiful shape and the cat who's selling it is the original owner. I'm going over to look at it tomorrow." He took a deep drag. "Want to come?"

"Sure," I said, "but you didn't come in here to lay that down."

He laughed, and took another hit. "I can see the studying has brought your mind to a keen edge, Peter," he said. "Well, what I wanted to know—" another hit "—fine dope, you sure you don't want any?"

"You wanted to know."

He laughed again. "Quite right," he said. "All business. I wanted to know if this chick is still up for doing it."

Then I remembered. "I meant to tell you," I said. "She

called last night and said she'd love to go to New York with you, but she's used up all her overnights."

"No, no," John said, "I meant—is that right? The little bitch. She called last night? I didn't know that. Why didn't you get hold of me?"

"You were in the rack with Sandra."

"Oh yeah," John said, remembering. "Oh yeah." He thought about it some more. "She can't go overnight? Jesus, that screws the whole weekend."

"Tell her that," I said.

He laughed, and then was silent, and finally said, as if remembering suddenly, "No, listen, I was talking about something else—that California chick, what's-her-name, does she still want to make a trip?"

That was surprising, even shocking. John's head was bent, but on one thing he was firm: he never changed his mind. Never, under any circumstances. I didn't know whether it was from obstinacy, or pride, or his Old Boston upbringing, but whatever the reason, it was true.

"Yeah, she'll do it." I didn't hesitate. I knew I could talk her into it—I'd almost done as much when the run wasn't even a sure thing. It was a way to come out and she wouldn't worry about it, if I said it was cool.

But I was interested in John's change of mind, in his sudden acceptance of Sukie. Hell, last time I'd talked to him he hadn't even considered the possibility.

"What happened?" I said. "Couldn't you find anyone else?"

John shrugged. "Well, let's see. You can't go because you fucked your exam. And everyone else's wonking their 'nads off for exams." He laughed. "Not doing a fucking thing, really, just sitting around chewing their nails. But if they're going to worry, they're going to do it here." He shook his head pityingly, then looked up at me. "The other thing is that Musty called and said he was leaving town for a while. He said if I wanted anything more before July, I had to do it now. So here we are." He smiled and took out another joint, lit it, passed it to me.

I took a long hit. "Musty's leaving town fast, huh?"

"That's the riff," said John.

"Far out," I said, and then laughed. Things had worked out better than I had hoped. I'd known that John would be pressed for a runner, but I didn't think he'd offer to let Sukie do it. I thought I'd have to cudgel him into it—and then here he was asking me if I thought she could make it. I laughed again. "Yeah, she'll do it."

"Good enough," said John. "Everything's set up, you'll send the money to Sukie and Musty's got the bricks ready. So all you've got to do is call the chick and let her in on it."

"Pretty sure of yourself, weren't you, John." It wasn't a question, it was a statement of fact. But John didn't take it that way. He waved the joint in my direction and said, "You were pretty sure of yourself, Peter." I guessed that he'd been figuring things out with Musty, and laughed.

"Yeah, I guess I was. But what the hell. She's coming. When will she fly in, anyway?"

"Saturday, around two."

I thought that one over and then realized what he had said.

"Saturday, good God. Not Saturday. I'm supposed to go to the Piggy Picnic on Saturday."

"Please. *Garden Party.*"

"Well, the hell with that. Annie Butler can blow her mind at me all she wants, I'm just not going to be able to make it. I'd better let her know as soon as I talk to Sukie——"

"Peter," said John. Nothing more.

"Yeah?"

"You're not going to tell Annie anything. I may have to let this chick make the run, but I don't have to let you two lovebirds fuck things up by prancing around Logan together, for every one of Murphy's pigs to see and admire."

"What the hell——"

"Murphy busted you in Berkeley, with the chick in the same room, right? And I expect that your mugs are fairly well known by the vice-squad pigs by now."

"Oh for Chrissake, get off it. Maybe my mug—maybe, if you really stretch it—but Sukie's, never. I'm going to go down and pick her up, and Annie Butler can go to hell."

John puffed slowly on what was by this time a dark roach. Finally he said, "This is my run and we're going to do it my way or not at all. You can tell the chick on the phone why you're not going to be there to meet her —but that's all. I'm not going to have this thing fucked up just to please your absurd sense of decorum, and that's all it is, Peter, so don't go making those bullshit faces at me. When the chick lands in Boston you're going to be having the time of your life at the Piggy

Club Garden Party. Period. I will be down at Logan waiting for her, and she'll be in the room about the time that you and Annie fondly bid each other farewell." He paused and looked at me. "Understand?"

There was nothing to say. I left the room to find a pay phone.

§

A surprised voice answered, sounding very far-away. It was a lousy connection. "Peter?"

"Yeah. How you doing, baby."

"Fine, just fine. Peter, God, it's good to hear from you."

I didn't say anything for a minute, just got stoned out of my mind on her voice, on the sound, knowing that in a few days the sound would be next to me and not coming through a piece of plastic that demanded more money every three minutes. Then I said, "Listen, honey. I've just been talking to John."

"John?"

"Yeah, you remember, my friend John back here, the guy I scored the bricks for when I was in Berkeley?"

"Oh." It wasn't noncommittal. It was just that she was beginning to understand. I had to keep it moving.

"Well, you remember that conversation we had, after my exam?"

"Yeah, I remember. Is this where John——"

"Just listen, honey, just let me finish. Things haven't been going too well for me around here. I mean, I've been trying to get some bread together so I could come out and see you again, or so you could come out here—you know, like the summer's getting here, and if we could get together we could do up the summer——"

"I'll do it, Peter." That was all she said.

"You don't mind? I mean, you know what I'm talking about——"

"I'll do it. I mind, but I'll do it. I want to see you."

I took a deep breath and it felt good. The chick was very, very together. "Okay, beautiful, honey that's beautiful. That's so beautiful, I can't even tell you. Listen, soon as you get here I'll take care of things, you know, a place to stay and eat and that whole riff, you don't worry about it, I'll work it all out. And then if you dig it around here we can do up the summer, you know, and——"

"Don't, Peter. You're blowing my mind. Just don't talk like that till I'm with you, okay?"

I knew what she was saying. "Okay, yeah, okay, you're right. Well, listen, I'll be sending the bread out to Musty tomorrow, and Musty'll know the details so he'll lay that end of it on you. The only other thing is that I won't be able to meet you at the airport." I had expected her to wonder about that, but all she said was, "That's cool."

"Out of sight. John'll meet you, he doesn't want me around 'cause of the bust but John'll meet you, and as soon as you get back to Cambridge I'll see you."

"That's cool."

Suddenly I didn't have anything more to say. I just wanted to see her, and talking business like this was only making it worse.

"Well——" I started to lay down something mindless, but she cut me off and said, "Peter. Take care of yourself."

I laughed at that. "I will baby. You do the same."

"Don't worry about me," she said. "You just be good." And then the operator was demanding more bread and she was saying goodbye and it was over.

As soon as I got back to the room I asked John where he'd put the dope.

"Gonna can the studying for a bit, Peter-old-boy?"

"Not can it, just enjoy myself before I get back on it."

John laughed. "Enjoy yourself, huh? You already look like you're enjoying yourself. You look like you just balled a nun, for Chrissake."

34

I was being shaken, quite hard, not a friendly shake at all. I opened my eyes and there was Annie Butler, all dressed up and looking very pretty except for her face, which was turned down.

"You're late," she said, as I opened my eyes.

"What?" I rubbed them.

"Late, you're late."

"What time is it?"

"One o'clock."

"Christ." I fell back in bed and groaned. I'd been up all night doing a paper and hadn't gotten to bed until dawn. I was wrecked.

"What are you doing?" she said.

"Going back to sleep."

"But the party," she said.

The party, Jesus. It all came back to me. I'd been

so intent on finishing the paper, so I wouldn't have to mess with it while Sukie was around, that I'd almost managed to forget about the party, the Piggy Club, the whole mess. I sighed.

"I'll wait in the living room while you dress," Annie said, and walked out. I sat up again and coughed. That's Annie. Three months later, she'll wait outside while you dress.

"Are you getting up?" she called from the living room.

"Yeah," I said.

"You going to shave?"

"Yeah, I'm going to shave."

"Good. You need it."

Charming as ever, dear Annie Butler. I went into the bathroom and turned on the shower.

"There isn't time for a shower, we're late already."

"I always shave in the shower," I said.

"Then hurry," Annie said. And finally, trailing afterward, like a dropping from a lame duck: "Please."

§

The garden party was held on a huge, rolling lawn, fenced in from the street and sheltered from its noise and plebeian curiosities by thick bushes. It was a gay scene, full of good cheer, and well stocked with food and drink. The lawn was dotted with colorful tables of food and booze; there was also a small army of polite, discreet, red-jacketed caterers.

The whole scene made me want to blow lunch. Since everyone in the Club knew that Annie Butler was Percy Pratfall's honey—or whatever the hell his name was—we'd had to make a great show of trotting around, greeting everyone, just to make sure they all understood on what grounds she'd managed to get in. She held my arm just tightly enough to show that I was her escort, and just loosely enough to show that I was her escort only for the afternoon. The pressure on my arm never changed, except when I would come out with something particularly obnoxious, when she'd give me a little squeeze of reproof. But I didn't really give a damn after the first half hour, since by then I had lost Annie and was doing my single-handed best to break the Piggy Club's liquor account wide open. And from the acid looks that the older members gave me, I knew that my efforts were not going unnoticed. After I'd discreetly managed to knock over five open hooch bottles and watched them gurgle and seep into the grass, one of the older members came over to demand that I produce my invitation card. This happened a number of times in the course of the afternoon—more often than would have been considered polite, in fact—and each time I produced my card, said something about boorish manners, and walked off. I got very drunk and a number of the members got very red in the face, and that was how it went. But I didn't mind the embarrassment of feeling that I didn't belong there; in fact, I rather enjoyed it. For the occasion I was wearing a pair of greasy blue jeans, a rumpled, plasticly-freaky shirt I'd gotten in the Village a few years before, a tired old blazer, and sneakers. Annie didn't care much for that, of course, but then, she could always have chosen not to go. She'd made her decision, and I'd made mine.

But as the afternoon wore on, the fun of hassling the old dudes wore off, and I was forced to hunt the really big game, which were the chicks. The chicks were all there, colorful dots on the rolling green lawn, just like the tables—and set up with the same cunning social design: to look so good that you'd want to take a bite, without knowing what you'd really bitten into. It was their only hope of survival, these chicks; they were like the kinds of insects you read about who have no natural defense except their bodily camouflage.

So I'd wander over to one of these chicks, and she'd go through her whole I'm-so-polite-and-interested-in-you routine, pausing to Ohh and Ahh whenever I said something that she figured was supposed to rate an Ohh or Ahh, and asking me if she could get anything for me at the buffet? This went on for as long as I could tolerate it. Then I would break down and start in on the old routine. It'd start when one of them stared at my clothes—politely, you understand, painfully politely, as though I'd been selected top boy in my Head Start class and been awarded an invitation to the Piggy Club Garden Party—and it would go on from there.

"My," she'd say, trying to giggle. "That certainly is a, well, a unique outfit you've got on there."

"Oh, you dig it? Hey, that's groovy to hear. You seem to be one of the few perceptive people here. Most of these creeps just stare at me like I'm some kind of bum."

Nobody had ever told her in her life that she was even remotely capable of being perceptive. "Oh," she'd say, "why, well ah . . ."

"You dig this scene?"

"Ah, well, you know . . ."

"That's what I thought. You're no dope. You're hip to what these creeps are putting down, I can see that."

"Well, I don't know, I don't know what to say, I mean . . ."

"What's your hustle around here anyway, honey? You dig? Who's throwing in the chips? You don't have to jive with me, baby. Just put it on me."

"Well, I, ah . . . I don't think I understand your question."

"Oh, a sly one, huh? Coming on slow, just to make me show my hand, huh? Come on, you're hip. What do you do around here?"

"You mean," she'd say, pointing her finger to the ground, "here?"

"Right, right, you're digging it."

"Ah, yes, I guess so, well, here, I mean right here, well, I'm a guest, I guess."

"A guest!" I'd guffaw loudly, and she'd look tremendously pleased that she'd said something funny. "A guest, *wow*. You got it, honey. That's far out. That's too much."

After a while she'd venture to say, "What're you doing here?"

"Me? Well, I don't know what I'm doing here right now, you dig? I mean, I could tell you why I thought I came here, but I don't know no more if that's what's happening or not, see?"

"Tell me," she'd say, "tell me, you can tell me."

"Well, like I came down here 'cause one of these creeps give my manager a ring, said he wanted a band to play this afternoon, down here. Dig it? So I came down. First thing I find out when I get here, they don't want no band. At least I don't think so, I mean nobody's said nothing to me about it so far——"

"You," she gulped her drink and pointed an astounded finger, "you play? In a band? A rock and roll band?"

"Shit, honey, I don't play in no shortwave band."

It'd be her turn to guffaw. "A shortwave band." Ha, ha!

"No, I mean, of course I play in a band. You might have heard our latest album on the radio, maybe. You ever listen to WBCN?" She'd shake her head yes, yes, all the time, of course she did. Of course, my ass. "Yeah, they got our latest album, you know, Lucifer Harkness and The New Administration. You remember that one? With the lead cut, remember that one, the lead song called 'The Cabinet Member,' and the guitar riff that goes dee-dee-dee, de dah, dee-dee-dee-dee deda dah, dwah, dwah, da duhn. Right? Can you dig it?"

"Gol-lee," she'd say, "that's you? That's your band? Gol-lee! I mean I never thought I'd ever actually meet you, and here, I mean, with all these . . . creeps."

That always got me. I'd guffaw.

"I thought you looked familiar. That must've been what it was—on your album cover, that big picture?"

"Right on," I'd say, "right on. Outasight. I knew you had it, honey, first time I seen you. Like you're the first chick here today's recognized me. Outasight."

"Gol-lee," she'd say.

I had to keep moving, though. The word got around amazingly fast, about the unknown celebrity in the greasy jeans who everyone'd been shitting on without knowing that he was really . . .

Who?

Finally it was four o'clock, and to my relief and the members' indescribable joy, I politely excused myself, regretting, to the ladies, that it looked after all as though I weren't going to be given a chance to play for them. They said it was a shame, I agreed it was a shame, and I made my escape.

On the way out, I looked around for Annie to say goodbye, but I didn't see her. I didn't look very hard.

35

I got back to the room just after four. I was a little bit smashed, but I didn't mind and I didn't figure that Sukie would. I kicked the door open, put my hands in my pockets, and walked in.

"Well, hi there," I said.

"Well, hi there," John said. "Bought the Lotus this morning. Magnificent machine. Got a pretty good trade-in on the Ferrari, too, better than I thought."

"Swell," I said, looking around.

No Sukie.

"I also got a place for the chick to stay," John said. "Sharon's old place. She's moved out, you know, and the rent's paid for another two weeks, and the furniture's still there, so . . ."

"Fine," I said, still looking.

"Don't thank me or anything, Peter-old-boy," John said. I looked over at him and realized that he was hugely pleased with himself for having lined up the place.

"Yeah, thanks, man, thanks. But where is she?"

"Here," John said, sprawling back on the couch and suddenly intensely interested in the new *Rolling Stone*.

"In Cambridge?"

"No, in Boston. She just called from the airport. Christ, that reminds me. What'd you give her our number for? You know I don't like——"

"Why did she call?"

John shrugged. "Some hang-up. They lost her bag."

"What bag," I said, but it wasn't a question. I just wanted to know what I was already afraid I knew.

"The bag with the grass." John sighed. He seemed to be taking it well. I couldn't believe he was just sitting there, telling me she'd lost the dope and sighing.

"The bag with the grass," I said. "Sweet Jesus, how could she lose that? It was under the goddamn seat——"

"No," said John. "She checked it."

"She what?"

"Checked it. It was a forty-brick run. You know as well as I do that if you're carrying forty bricks, you're gonna have to check one of the bags."

"You didn't tell me it was going to be that big a——"

"You didn't ask," John said, slipping back into his magazine. He was again suddenly fascinated by the magazine, the bastard. From behind it he said, "Anyway, she'll be okay. She said they just lost it somewhere in transit."

"In transit, my ass," I said. "What did you tell her to do?"

"I told her to go back and get it."

36

I had to sit down for a minute to think that one out, it was so unbelievable. And then I found that I couldn't think, that I was so pissed that I couldn't do anything but shout at John and tell him what I thought about sending the chick back. He just sat and stared at me and said nothing and finally I realized that I was wasting precious time. Bag or no bag, if I could get to Sukie before they did . . . "Where're the keys to the Lotus?"

"Give me back the *Rolling Stone*," John said. I'd ripped it out of his hands without knowing what I was doing, and as I handed it back he gave me the keys. "Don't run it over forty-five-hundred revs," he yelled after me, as I hustled out the door, "it's just had a valve job."

§

All the way out to the airport I ground the gears and ran it over forty-five-hundred revs. Fucking John, he'd really screwed me this time, screwed me so bad that I couldn't believe it was happening—that he'd just let it happen. The dude had a loose bolt somewhere, especially when it came to chicks. Or other people. Or other people's chicks. I mean, what the hell was the cat thinking of, sending Sukie back for the bag. Because he knew about running dope, and he knew about "lost" bags at the airport. This wasn't the first time we'd ever "lost" a bag. The first time had cost John a pretty penny, to buy Jeffrey off, and we'd all learned from the experience. Ever since then, we'd had strict rules for runs, especially runs which involved bags in the hold. First, no matching sets of luggage. Second, no name tags. Third, no real names used on tickets, so that nothing could be traced from the baggage check on a busted bag. Fourth, the specially designed, double-locked, lined bags, which made it impossible for the heat to open the bags without irreparably breaking them and so disqualifying any potential evidence on the grounds of illegal search and seizure.

Those were the first four rules, and the fifth was never to go back for a lost bag. Because it just meant trouble and time in court and a hell of a lot of money. We never went back for a "lost" bag, because these days the narcs didn't always have to open a bag to find the stuff. The narcs were into all kinds of things now: dogs trained to growl at the smell of dope, even dope soaked in Coca-Cola and wrapped in aluminum; and odor-analyzers, weird little machines with a sort of gun attachment that sniffed the air and lit up when they smelled dope.

And so anything that we put in the hold was a strictly calculated risk, and not something to be toyed with. Because the heat had their own little hustle: when they'd catch a bag full of weed, they'd hold it, announce that it was lost, and then bust whoever showed up to claim it. Not a very original hustle—and anybody who's carrying always knows that if they say your bag is lost, *split.* Split fast and never go back. But Sukie'd never run any dope before, and so she'd called John and asked him what to do. And John——

Fucking John.

I hot-assed it through Sumner tunnel, paid my toll, and blasted up the ramp toward the airport—only to come to a dead halt twenty yards up the road. Airport traffic. Newsboys sauntered in and out among the rows of cars with maddening assurance that nobody was going anywhere. Hawking the Boston papers, the most provincial newspapers in America ("Saugus Man Dies in New York Nuclear Holocaust") and the crookedest (look at page ten for the small item "Ten Officials Indicted in 44 Million Swindle") as befits the town. I sat in the car and swore and lit a cigarette and got paranoid. My head was completely spaced. I couldn't even remember if Sukie had come in on United or TWA. Most of all, I couldn't figure out what John had been trying to do when he'd sent her back. Because if anyone knew how much it'd cost to buy her off of a forty-brick rap, he did. American justice is extraordinarily expensive; the bribe must always measure up to the crime. Forty bricks was going to set John back quite a ways, if anything happened to Sukie.

If anything happened to Sukie . . .

I had visions of arriving just as they were slapping the cuffs on her, of a fleeting glance of her face looking over her shoulder, looking at me sadly the way she had that night they had dragged me away. She was showing no reproach and somehow that made it worse. And then suddenly she was at the end of a long hallway, it was somewhere in Berkeley but I knew that the hallway would look the same no matter where it was, fluorescent lights leering, and she had on a gray sack dress and two matrons were taking her, still cuffed, down a flight of stairs. I watched helplessly and saw again the sad, unreproachful face over the shoulder.

Then the line started moving and I began thinking about lawyers and bail bondsmen and where in the world I was going to scrape up the bread. I drifted out of my lane and some swine in a Cadillac honked and skinned my front fender in a burping burst of exhaust. Fuck you, fella. I was down the ramp and at the airport and parked in a cab zone before I knew it. A cop shouted at me that I'd have to move, but I just ran inside, past the people and the porters and the heat that seemed to be everywhere, wondering why I'd never noticed how many heat hung around the place.

I knew where the lost-bag rooms were, and I decided to try United first. I sprinted down a long corridor, turned a corner, and found the office. There was nobody there. TWA's depot was just a little farther on down, so I decided to check it out, then return to United if nothing was happening there. But the seemingly endless construction that was always going on at Logan had transformed TWA's lost-bag office into a coffee shop, so I stopped a porter and asked him where it had gone.

"I just flew in on TWA and they've lost one of my bags," I said. "Where do I find it?"

"TWA's baggage over there," he shrugged, pointing around a corner. I ran over, and stopped in front of a door which said MISCELLANEOUS, AUTHORIZED PERSONNEL ONLY. The door was open but partially blocked by a low table, and inside there were racks and racks of bags, bags of all kinds, bags everywhere.

And standing knee-deep in this ocean of bags was Sukie. On each side of her was a man in a raincoat. One of them was putting on the cuffs and before I could turn away and get out of there I saw the tight, familiar, ugly neck, heard the rough, humorless voice. And knew that Murphy had busted another freak.

3
A Taste of Soup

If a fool be associated with
a wise man even all his life,
he will perceive the truth as
little as a spoon perceives
the taste of soup.

THE DHAMMAPADA

You can steal my chickens
But you can't make 'em lay.

WILLIE DIXON

37

I was back out in the Lotus and on my way back to Cambridge before I really thought about what I was doing. And even when I did start thinking, it was only about one thing: John, and the shit I was going to knock out of him. I hadn't been able to understand, on the way to Logan, why he'd sent Sukie back; but now I didn't care. He was alone when I found him in the room, and he didn't even look up when I came in. He was tearing the place apart. The radio was on, giving the weather report. John was pulling out dresser drawers, removing the bricks that were taped to the back.

I just stared at him.

"Well," he said, "let's get it on."

"Get what on, half-ass?"

John stopped and looked at me. "You're alone, right? So the chick's busted, right? So let's get it on and get this place cleaned up, so we can get out of here."

I froze. "You bastard. This wouldn't have happened if you hadn't sent——"

"This wouldn't have happened, Peter, if your chick hadn't already given the pigs her name, her Berkeley address, and our Cambridge telephone number before she thought to call me up and ask what she should do about her 'lost bag.' So I told her to go back. What the hell, why not? It didn't make any difference at that point."

"She gave them our phone number?"

"Yeah," John said. "That's a smart little pussy you've got. She really set us up—you with your record—your *recent* record—and me holding."

"She didn't know . . ."

"And you didn't tell her, did you? That's why she didn't know. You didn't tell her the first goddamn thing about it."

"I didn't know she'd have to check a bag——"

"The fuck you didn't. You sent her a check for ten thousand. That's forty bricks. You just overlooked it, you were in such a ball-crushing rush——"

"Now listen, brother, you talk like that, you're gonna have to pay some dues. I sent her the check, yeah, but I didn't know——"

"Help me clean this place out," John said in a voice that was final. He was throwing the bricks onto the center of the floor.

I still couldn't get very excited about John's problems. "Listen, man, you don't seem to be digging what's happened to the chick. She's in jail, for Chrissake, and——"

"And we won't be any good to her," John said, taking out the jars and bottles from the medicine cabinet, "if we're in there with her. Now come on."

We cleaned the place out. All together, we found sixteen bricks of good smoking dope, a hundred caps of synthetic mescaline, five hundred and fifty caps of psilocybin, thirteen peyote buttons in cellophane, four ounces of hash, and some Thorazine. John got one of his friends to drive it out in a couple of suitcases to John's uncle's house in Lexington.

When that was done we both had a big belt of his

Scotch. The room was disordered; John kicked some clothes off the couch and sat down. "If Murphy busted her, you'd better do what I'm doing," he said. "Take off for a day or two, at least stay away from this room. It's not going to be too cool for a while."

I didn't give a shit how cool it was, I had other things on my mind. "Look," I said, "we've got to get her out of jail as fast as we can. She won't know what to say, and she'll fuck herself over in a matter of hours without some advice. If we can't get her out and talk to her before the arraignment on Monday, she won't know enough to plead guilty. And if that happens, the case'll go up through the courts, dig?"

"Yeah," said John. He was digging it. He was digging the fact that if that went down, we'd never be able to buy her off, no matter what lawyer we eventually got for her. And she'd take the full rap for the bust, probably even do some time. I waited for John to say something, to figure something out. There was a very long pause, and then he just said, "Yeah."

"Yeah, what?"

John looked pained, really pained, for the first time since I'd walked in the door. "Peter," he said. "The pigs have overvalued the bust, as usual. They've announced that they picked up fifteen-thousand-dollars' worth of dope. So that means it'll cost us at least three thousand to get her off. Plus her bail, which as you have noticed is essential. Now. I don't know if her bail's been set yet, but you can bet your ass it'll be at least ten thousand. So that's another grand we need right there——"

"So?"

"So this is Saturday," John said.

"What the hell does that have to do with anything?"

"The market's closed."

"Now wait a minute. Are you trying to tell me you're broke? You?"

"I'm saying I won't have a nickel until Monday." John paused, then added, "After ten o'clock."

I couldn't believe he'd said that. I couldn't believe any of the things that had gone down that afternoon, but that was the end. Finally I said, "Far out." Nothing more.

John nodded. "It is far out. It's a drag, too, but it's what's happening. I'll do everything I can. But I can't do anything till Monday."

"Far out," I said again. Then, almost as an afterthought, "You son of a bitch."

"Peter," John said slowly, "it's all I can do. It's all I can do." He got up and put on his jacket. On the way out he paused and said, "If you want me for anything, I'll be at Sandra's."

Then the door closed, and I was alone.

38

The first thing I did was pour myself three fingers of John's J & B, put on some blues, and sit down to try to get my head together. Which was easier said than done. I was flashing on all the things that had gone down, on all the ridiculous little twists and turns the trip had taken in the course of a few hours. Sukie busted.

Murphy on our backs again. John broke—that was what really blew my mind, that John could be broke. It was too much. Finally I realized that I wasn't getting anywhere, that I had to get ripping or I'd just drown. But I just sat there, immobilized.

The worst thing in the world is not to be moving when you've got to move, when you've got to do something. Like hitching. I used to hitch a lot, whenever I was desperate to get moving. Once when I was bumming around Vermont I ran into this fag, an old guy who was really hurting for somebody to come-on to. He picked me up, wanted to know where I was going, and I just said, Wherever you are. Which was all he needed to get it on. Before I knew it we were off the road and at his house, and he said I should go on in and make myself comfortable, he had a few phone calls to make.

His place looked as though no one had ever lived there, full of broken furniture and old newspapers. The guy was on the phone a long time, so after a while I went into the can to take a leak. I'd just gotten it out when he popped his head in the door. His eyes lit up when he saw me and then he casually sauntered in and started brushing his teeth. I didn't have the faintest idea what was going down, so I continued about my business. Suddenly he pops his head up from the bowl and asks me if I've ever been blown. I didn't think so, I replied. Well, he demanded, wouldn't I like to try it out now? I mean, after all, if I'd never tried it, I didn't have the slightest idea what I was missing. I said No thanks, I didn't want to try. The whole scene had suddenly become bizarrely comic, as I'd realized why he was brushing his teeth. The dude was being polite. He was letting me know that, hygienically at least, he wasn't a dirty old man.

And he wasn't about to give up so easily, either. Was I sure I didn't want to try it out? Honest-to-goodness sure? 'Cause he'd noticed—no harm in looking, see—he'd noticed that I wasn't circumscribed, and did I know how much more sensitive that made me? Circumcised, I thought he meant. Circumscribed, circum-shmibed, what difference did it make—didn't I want to try?

No, sorry, I didn't, and maybe I'd just better be going, if he had finished making his phone calls. And then all of a sudden he was blocking the door, and I was realizing that he wasn't so old, and that he was pretty big to boot. So I picked up the nearest thing at hand, which was a plumber's helper, and asked him if he was going to get out of the way, feeling ridiculous even as I did so. Knock the fag around in his own can with his own plumber's helper. It was too much. Suddenly I started to laugh. I couldn't believe it, but I laughed and laughed and laughed, until I dropped the plumber's helper; and I kept laughing long after he'd shaken his head in dumb amazement and walked out.

By the time I stopped laughing he'd brought the car around front, and was all ready to drive me back to the highway. On the way he suddenly started rapping. Seemed the dude was married, had a few kids, held down a regular job. But he just couldn't have enough of that old Get you, Gertrude, so he'd rented the second house for practically nothing, and he went out every night picking up hitchhikers. I asked him how he did. He said that now and then he found himself a goodie, but usually they were like me. You mean No Go, I said. Well, at first, he said, but then he'd hassle them in the can, and they'd get tough and knock him around. It suddenly dawned on me that this was the whole point of that scene. They'd knock him around, and then he'd cry and apologize, and then they'd be sorry, and then half the time, it turned out, they'd feel so bad they'd wind up letting him work them over.

He was about to go on when I asked him why he did things that way. I meant that if he was a fag, why not be one full-time? Why screw around working the night shift when you've got the whole day, too. But he didn't understand me that way, and what came back was a jumbled, confused defense of his wife, and the kids, and his place in the community.

Why didn't he just split? I kept asking. Oh no, was all he'd say. He couldn't do that. After all, that'd been his life for twenty years. To quit now would be ridiculous, totally ridiculous. Be a fag? Of course not. Nobody would ever buy shoes from him again. His wife would probably leave him. The kids would look at him funny.

I began to see things differently after that. I began to notice how much people treasured their solidity, their immobility. It made everything safe. And what I noticed now, on my third shot of John's J & B, was that I was into the same riff. I was a student—that was my gig—and even though I put it down, I was completely into ripping it off for all it was worth. I didn't mind getting busted in Berkeley, because there I was just another dude. But to have Sukie busted on my turf, in my town, where I was cool—well, that just didn't make it. It didn't make it at all, and instead of trying to do something about it I just sat around and waited for somebody to bail me out.

I started over to grab another hit of J & B, paused, and sat down. It was up to me now, as it had always been. I simply hadn't wanted to look it in the face. If Sukie was still in jail at the arraignment, she'd be up the river; and even if I got her out before then, there was still a chance that she'd go up unless I got her a lawyer as well. I had to do something.

So I dialed O'Leary's office and demanded to speak to someone, anyone. But I only got a half-witted chick on answering service, who informed me that it was Saturday and everyone was home. Would I please call back Monday? How about home phones, I wanted to know. Well, that depended. Was I a client already? Or was I simply seeking information? No, she was sorry, if I wasn't already a client she wasn't permitted to give me any home phones. Lawyers had to sleep, just like everyone else. The office would be open on Monday at nine.

Thank you, bitch. What next? I called up all the bail bondsmen I could find in the book. They had not gone home—they did a thriving business on Saturday night, that much was obvious. But no, they wouldn't accept a stereo as collateral on a ten-thousand-dollar bond, it wouldn't be worth it to them, and anyway they'd been getting too many stolen goods for collateral lately. They were taking only large items they could be sure of, like cars, these days. *Click.*

I poured myself another Scotch, got thoroughly sloshed, and turned on the television to catch the evening news. As it came on, Herbie showed up; he was on his way to dinner and was looking for company. I said I wasn't hungry but offered him a drink, and he sat down to watch the news with me.

After the usual Vietnam-Central-American-coup-Middle-East-retaliation-domestic-upheaval reports, they came to the local news. And to Susan Blake, a nineteen-year-old resident of San Francisco, California, arrested today at Logan Airport on charges of possession of marijuana. Her suitcase was found to contain forty pounds of marijuana. She will be arraigned Monday. Elsewhere in the city . . .

"Far out," Herbie said.

"Yeah," I said.

He laughed. "Well," he said, nodding to the TV, "you don't have to take it personally, just because somebody gets busted."

I looked over at him. "Herbie," I said, "that's my chick."

There was a long pause while Herbie thought that one over, and I thought that one over. Then Herbie said again, "Far out."

I didn't say anything.

"What're you going to do?"

I shook my head. "I've got to get bail for her. I've got to get her out of there."

"That means money," Herbie said.

"Yeah." I got up, a little unsteadily, and went into the bedroom to get some cigarettes. When I came out, Herbie was still there, staring at me with a quizzical look on his face.

"How are you going to do it?"

I shrugged. "Your bet's as good as mine."

Herbie laughed. "In other words," he said, "you don't have any idea."

I didn't laugh. Herbie was right.

39

Later that night it began to rain, cold, streaky splatterings against the window, as I stared out at the courtyard. I was wrecked but I was still trying to think of something to do for Sukie. I had been in tight places before, especially when I'd been doing my own dealing. One time in Berkeley a good friend of mine had been busted, busted so badly that if I hadn't come up with some bread for a lawyer he would have done a couple of years. But getting that bread had been something else—something I just wasn't up for, this time around.

It was spring—a warm spring, I remembered, staring out at the rain—and I had been so enchanted with Berkeley and the people I'd met, that I'd just kept putting off the business part of my trip. And then, the morning that I was definitely going to see about business, Steven announced that we were going to Big Sur and loaded his VW bus full of camping equipment and charming chicks, and off we had gone, my feeble protests notwithstanding. So that it wasn't until my last day in town that I had gone to see Ernie, the connection in those days.

I'd found Ernie lying on the living room floor of his gaudily painted apartment, stoned out of his mind on psilocybin. And Ernie had informed me, in rather vague but nonetheless emphatic terms, that there was no grass to be had, at least not down his alley. The gist of our conversation was more accurately that he told me to get the hell out of his place, he was stoned on psilocybin and didn't want to get bummed on dope deals. That night I'd found out about my friend's bust, and it was then that I'd decided to do some instant hustling on my own.

The next day I went out on the street. Walked down to the Forum and stood around, just listening, waiting for something to happen. Asking anybody who looked like they knew which way was up if they had any bricks, and always getting No for an answer, but always with a few references ("Shit man, nothing happening far as I know, but you could ask Toad—you know that dude, Toad, wild-looking freak with four fingers on one hand, he's always up around here about six. He had some bricks last week"). And waiting around to ask Toad, and Sonny, and Detroit Danny, and anybody else that might show up.

And then finally, just when I was about to leave, say the hell with it, and climb back onto the Beantown bird, these four black cats showed up and started talking bricks. And everybody jumped, because Ernie had been, in his own way, telling the truth. There just wasn't that much dope to be had. So everybody on the street was hungry to get their hands on weed, and they were taking chances they wouldn't ordinarily take, like fronting bread to strangers, in the hope of scoring some smoke and being the only cat in town with, as the saying goes, shit to burn.

Which set up these four spades, who wouldn't normally have had a prayer of hustling dope on the Avenue. They were flashy dressers, all conked and zooted, and they looked to be as likely prospects for bricks as a Central Square car salesman. But everybody else seemed to trust them; everybody else was fronting bread to them and dreaming mounds and mounds of dope, so I dreamed too, and we arranged to meet and exchange commodities.

I went off to wait in a supermarket parking lot, and pretty soon a huge white Caddy snaked in and I hopped on board. They didn't know Berkeley, they said, they'd just driven a load up from San Diego because they'd heard things were dry. So we drove around for a while, looking for a good place to do the deal. The whole time, all they could say was "What's a cool place? Find a cool place, man, a cool place." They seemed very nervous and jumpy, which I thought a good sign, a sign they really had stuff. I kept them driving around for a long time in search of the mythical cool place.

I wasn't about to tell them I didn't know Berkeley any better than they did, because I didn't want them to think I didn't know what I was doing. Dope dealing, especially when buyer and seller are unacquainted, involves a primitive ritual which can be described in terms of I Am More Hip Than Thou. The object, if you are buying, is to let the other cat know (never directly but as forcefully and significantly as possible) that (1) you have bought a lot of dope in your time, and are not to be messed with; (2) you know what dope goes for in the area, and what quality it should be for the price; and, hopefully, (3) you are a very big dealer yourself and can provide the seller with a lot of business if he measures up to your standards.

Now all this is for real, and deadly serious at the time it's going on, simply because the margins for profit are so broad and so extraordinarily ill-defined for both parties. For example, the seller knows that he can deal a good brick in Berkeley for about a hundred and twenty-five bucks, but he may have paid fifty, seventy-five, or even a hundred for that brick himself, depending on where he bought it and in what quantity. So he may or may not be in a position to be talked into lowering his price. On the other hand, if the seller discovers that you, the buyer, are not from Berkeley but from the East Coast, and consequently will not have to be competitive in terms of California prices when you unload the bricks, the seller's price will shoot right up. So both sides play an intense strong-arm psychological game, and I was working hard at it when we got to one quiet, lazy street and I motioned them over to the side.

"This a cool street, man?"

"Yeah, very cool," I said. And then, "In fact, I live here. I just wanted to do it here so I wouldn't have to walk around the streets holding." They laughed nervously. "Let's get out and check those bricks," I said. The keys were supposed to be in the trunk. I started to get out when a quick, leathered arm pulled me back.

"Be cool, brother. I'll get the stuff."

Be cool. Yeah, groovy. Only I didn't dig "being cool" in the car, because I was holding a fuck of a lot of bread and they'd seen it. And so long as I stayed in the car it was too easy a set-up. I'd shown them my bread but I hadn't seen any bricks, and I was alone with four cats I didn't know. So when the cat hopped out I stuck my boot in the door, then kicked it open and followed him back to the trunk.

"Thought I told you to stay in the car, man. You want to fuck us up?"

"Relax, man," I said, "relax. Nobody's going to fuck anybody up. I'm just doing what I came here to do. Now let's see those bricks."

He looked at me suspiciously and then nodded and opened the trunk. That's a good sign, I thought, as he disappeared into the trunk, that's a good sign, that he's so nervous. He's as uptight about getting ripped off as I am and that means he must have the shit.

He emerged holding a small brown-paper bag. There were supposed to be four bricks in the bag and it didn't look big enough for two, but I figured, What the hell, what the hell, the market's tight and he's probably got pound-and-a-half bricks. He wouldn't have told me beforehand because he'd be afraid I wouldn't want them, but what the hell, I'll take pound-and-a-half bricks before I'll go home empty-handed, and maybe we can arrange a lower price or something. At any rate, I was still with him as he placed the bag of bricks on the roof of the Caddy and turned to me. I was still with him and events were moving along now like a poker game. After every round the spade would look over to see if I was still in the game.

"Let's see them," I said.

"You got all day to look at them bricks," he said. "How's about you handing over the bread?"

The stakes were going up. "I just want to have a quick look," I said.

And then I pulled out my knife, a little Swiss Army knife that I always carried with me to cut the bricks open and slice off a taste.

The spade had been looking nervously in the direction of the other three dudes in the car, and when he turned to me and saw the knife he jumped back in fright.

"Hey man!" he was almost yelling. "What'chu doing, huh? What'chu doing? Put that blade away, man! Put it away right now or the deal's off." He stood back away from me as he talked, as if I'd threatened to stick him with it when I'd taken it out.

"Relax for Chrissake," I said. "I'm going to cut a taste and then you can get out of here."

"How 'bout the bread, man," he said, still keeping his distance from the blade. "How 'bout the bread. You got the bricks now how 'bout the bread!"

I told him to relax again and reached for the bag, knife out to cut the string, and all of a sudden he was banging on the roof of the Caddy, banging hard and the doors were opening and I suddenly realized why he'd been so paranoid about the knife, if he hadn't been trying to rip me off he wouldn't have given a goddamn about the knife. He wouldn't have even been thinking about the knife. He would've been shitting in his pants because of an insane honky who was insisting on tasting his bricks in broad daylight, on a side street just three blocks off Telegraph, a side street that the heat could come down at any moment, just casually cruising, the heat, and then I knew what was happening, knew and it was unbelievable that I'd walked into it as alone and blind as I had. The four of them were standing around me now and they had their hands in their pockets and before they could get them out I was talking.

"Listen, man, you digging that window, that window over there, that ground-floor window, my brother lives in there and right now he's got a forty-four trained right on your fucking head, you dig? You mess with me and the dogs around here gonna be munching your guts for dinner, you dig? Right in that ground floor window over there my brother——"

And as I talked two of the dudes had their hands out of their pockets and I was staring down two shiny silvered .38s, thinking, Ugly, ugly, this can't have happened to me, this isn't real, I didn't walk into a set-up like this, I mean, I couldn't have, this just can't be real—thinking, This is real, it must be real, those guns are ugly, they're pointed right at my fucking guts, this has got to be real and I've got to get out of here before it gets any more real—

thinking, I know this can't be real, I know it's not real, it's happening so fast, all of it, but I've got to get out of here so fast before it is real—

thinking, Suddenly I'm getting my ass out of here before I'm not around anymore to dig how real it is; and then out of nowhere I started yelling, yelling my lungs out, not daring to look at the spades, yelling at the window yelling

"Zeph, hey Zeph, *Zeph, these boys are looking for trouble, show 'em where you're at in there, Zeph*" and I kept right on yelling, and the dudes were looking at each other and getting a little more nervous, and then it happened.

Whoever the hell he was, he saved my skin. Some scared little guy pulled back the curtain in the ground-floor apartment and gave me one of those Crazy Kids looks and dropped the curtain again. And that was just enough of a pause for me. I grabbed the paper bag off the roof and ran faster than I'd ever known I could run, down underneath an apartment house through the garage and running my ass off, waiting the whole time to catch something hot and sharp in the small of my back, running and waiting and running for what seemed an eternity, running up to an eight-foot fence and right over it into a backyard on the next street over.

I couldn't believe I'd made it. I took a deep breath, but the situation had me flowing with its energy and before I'd even thought about what had happened I had the bag open and was staring at a pair of sneakers wrapped in T-shirts. I dropped the bag and went back up to Telegraph to badmouth those cats. The whole number lasted maybe twenty minutes.

Give or take ten years.

40

I didn't want to get into that kind of scene again, but I didn't know what else to do. So finally I went to see if Herbie was still up and about, and I found him wide-eyed and stoned out of his mind but ready to rip.

"I thought you'd show," Herbie said as I came into the room. "Want to get some breakfast?"

I was surprised. "It's that late?"

"Yeah." He checked his watch. "Seven-thirty." He stepped out the door, and came back in holding the morning paper. "Your old lady ought to have gotten a big write-up," he said. "Big splash." He sighed. "Wish I could help," he said, "but . . ."

I nodded. There was nothing he could do. Obviously, there was nothing that any of us could do. "A forty-brick bust," I said. "That's a hell of a big bust."

"She got anything else going for her?" Herbie said.

"No prior offenses, no record," I said. "That's something."

He nodded. "College student?"

"No."

"Too bad. Work history? Can she prove she doesn't do this for a living?"

"She hasn't worked at some job for five years, if that's what you mean."

"Psychiatric history?"

"Nothing," I said. That was the last resort, so far as defense went, but for young defendants it often helped.

Herbie sighed again, and shook his head. Then he looked up suddenly. "How many bricks did you say?"

"What?"

"How many bricks was she busted for holding?"

"Forty," I said.

"Forty kilos?"

"That's what I said."

"That's odd," Herbie said. As I'd been talking he'd

been leafing through the paper. "Because it says here . . . wait a minute . . . dadadadedah . . . umm. . . . Here. It says 'Susan Blake, busted for forty pounds in twenty kilos.' "

"Well, they made a mistake," I said. "Fucking newspapers can't even get the facts on a goddamn local bust down right. Anyway," I shrugged, "it was forty keys."

Herbie stared at the paper some more. "No," he said.

"No, what?"

"No, they did not make a mistake. The sentence is internally consistent. Forty pounds would be just under twenty kilograms. That's accurate."

"Yeah, well, she had forty keys, forty bricks——"

"What did they say on the news last night?"

I shrugged. "I don't remember."

"Well," Herbie said, "it's important, because if it's only twenty keys, her bail might be lower."

"Far out," I said, and felt momentarily encouraged. Until I began to think of some other things that I had never thought of. Things I should have considered right off, especially with Murphy involved.

"Herbie," I said, "this is far out. This is very far out." Herbie looked interested. "Dig it: I *know* that there were forty keys in that shipment. Sukie was holding down two suitcases, twenty keys to a suitcase. Total value, ten thousand dollars. I mailed the check to her myself."

"That is far out," Herbie said. "The boys in blue seem to have gotten pretty arrogant." He smiled, and buried his nose in the newspaper. " 'Cause it says here 'one suitcase,' and that means that . . . Where do you think it's being dumped?"

"Roxbury," I said, "or Somerville. That's a beginning, anyway."

"Okay," Herbie said, getting off on the whole idea of fucking up the pigs. "Now we need a car, and binoculars. I have both. Also, we have to stop off at the drugstore . . ."

"What?"

"I'll meet you in the courtyard in ten minutes," Herbie said on his way out the door.

41

An hour later we found ourselves in Herbie's VW, parked across the street from District Station House Number Four. It was still raining slightly, and on a Sunday afternoon this part of town, on the east edge of Roxbury, was quiet. Herbie gave me the binoculars. "Here," he said "You're the one who knows what he looks like."

I took the binoculars and tried to look through them. Herbie had focused them for his own eyes, and they were completely blurred for me. While I changed the focus, Herbie took off his glasses and wiped them on his tie. "You know," he said conversationally, "Boston has the lowest pay scales for police of any place in the country."

"That right?" I said. I was now focused on the front steps.

"Yes," Herbie said. "That's what's behind it all. That and the mail."

"The mail?" I repeated, still looking through the binoculars. A man came out of the station, talking to a cop in uniform. The man wasn't Murphy.

"Yes," Herbie said. "Cops get mail just like everybody else. Last year's murder rate in Boston went up sixty percent over the year before. But the mail doesn't say 'Stop the murders.' The mail says 'Get those nasty kids with their nasty drugs.' "

"Oh," I said.

Another man came out of the station. He wasn't Murphy, either. I sighed.

"Better relax," Herbie said, lighting a joint and passing it to me. "It could be a long time. You know, you can't really blame them."

"Who?"

"Whom. The police," Herbie said. "Dope is money, you know. Why not make a little extra?"

"Yeah," I said. And I added, "I hope Murphy's broke."

"That probably isn't the motivating factor," Herbie said. He said it in a cryptic, dry way and I suddenly flashed on what Herbie was doing here: weak, nearsighted, brilliant little Herbie, who was still working up to his first Big Date at the age of seventeen. Herbie was here because it was a manipulation trip, action at a distance, control from afar, guess and second-guess, with cops-and-robbers overtones. He was playing it hot and heavy, and loving every minute of it.

"I'm going to work on the gun," he said, and leaned into the back seat to get it.

One hour passed, then two, then three. I began to get depressed. It seemed that things like this were always coming down on me, waiting things, dependent things,

things where I wasn't in control and had to bide my time, see what developed. It happened to everybody, of course, but that didn't make it any better. Waiting to get out of high school so you could get away from Main Street. Waiting to get your degree so you could go out and wait for a job. Waiting for the bank loan. Waiting for the kids to grow up. Waiting for the draft to blow your neck. Waiting for the record to end—the same dismal, crummy record that played the same dismal, crummy song over and over, the song that went "When does it end, and who is it that's won, and will I die, too, before it's begun?"

Three and a half hours later the VW seemed very cramped, the air very stale. Herbie said he'd go across the street to a sandwich shop and get a couple of subs, while I stayed with the binoculars. He asked me what I wanted and I said a meatball sandwich. He came back with it for me, and it was terrible, a true crapball concoction, to be washed down by an artificially flavored, artificially colored beverage of some sort. I frowned when I bit into it and he asked me if it was what I had wanted. It wasn't, of course. I thought about how I could never seem to get what I wanted. Nobody in America could, for that matter, unless of course you happened to want something that you could purchase, in which case you had an immense variety of guaranteed satisfactions. But even that had been going on too long. Too many people had been getting all the new cars and the new tubes and the new refrigerators that they'd wanted for so long. And now they wanted something else. But they didn't know what.

Four hours passed.

Herbie got the latest papers, to see if there was more about Sukie or the size of the bust. There wasn't.

Another half hour.

And then, suddenly, stepping out into the afternoon light, rubbing the bald spot on the back of his head, was The Pig. "Herbie," I said, "that's him."

Herbie put down the paper. "What's six letters meaning determination?"

I pointed to Murphy, walking alone down the steps with a small briefcase in one hand. "That's him."

"Well, what are you waiting for?" Herbie said. "Let's get going."

I started the engine, and put the VW in gear.

42

Murphy drove a green Plymouth sedan. It was dusty and needed to be washed, and it had the usual 415 narc plates. Murphy climbed in and carefully put on a large pair of Highway Patrol-type shades, and then started off.

I followed the car through the Boston traffic. As we went, I said, "Herbie, there's one problem."

"There are no problems," Herbie said flatly.

"Yes," I said, "there's one: what if he's already unloaded the stuff? What if he unloaded it last night?"

"That's not a problem," Herbie said. "That's a factor we've taken into account."

"We have?"

"Yes. It's been perfectly clear from the start that if he has already unloaded the dope, or if he's not the one who's doing it, then we are wasting our time."

"Oh," I said.

Murphy drove to the South End of town, pulled up at a bus stop, parked, and got out. I pulled over beside a hydrant a few yards back. We watched Murphy go into a church.

"I don't like it," Herbie said.

"Why?" I said.

"He's taking that briefcase with him," Herbie said, getting out of the car. I started to follow him. "No," Herbie said, "not you. He'd recognize you."

So I got back into the car and waited while Herbie scurried up to the church, and disappeared inside. Several minutes passed. I turned on the radio but all I could get was Connie Francis singing "Who's Sorry Now?" and some damned symphony. I turned the radio off and smoked a cigarette. Several more minutes passed. I turned the radio back on. This time I found a talk show, with Tony Curtis. They asked Tony whether he thought he was successful and Tony said it depended on how you defined it. He defined success as doing better than his best friend. And he said he was successful, on that basis. He didn't name the best friend.

Then Murphy came out of the church, still carrying the briefcase. Herbie was nowhere to be seen. Murphy got into his car, threw the briefcase into the back seat, started the engine, and waited. I watched him, wondering where Herbie was, and why Murphy was waiting.

At that moment, Herbie came out of the church, moving very fast. I glanced over at Murphy. Murphy was looking at Herbie. Christ, I thought, it's all over. Herbie jumped into the seat next to me. "All set," he said. "Why's he waiting?"

"Don't know," I said. But then I saw him lean forward, take out the dashboard lighter, and light the cigarette between his lips. I sighed. "There's your answer. Just getting a nic hit."

At that moment, Murphy took off. He patched out, leaving a blue cloud of exhaust and the smell of rubber, and streaked down the street.

"Shit," I said, slamming the car into gear.

"I wonder what he has under that hood," Herbie said thoughtfully.

Murphy was now moving very fast, heading toward the Expressway. He went up the ramp and I followed him, running a red light to make it. "What was he doing in the church?"

"Praying," said Herbie.

Murphy screamed forward onto the Expressway. He wove among the lanes of traffic, trying to lose us.

The VW didn't have enough power to touch the Plymouth, which moved steadily away from us. For a while, Herbie was able to keep track of him with the binoculars, while I took some bad chances, slipping in and out among the cars. But finally, near Milton, we came over a rise in the Expressway and looked down over the far slope, and he was gone.

Completely gone.

Herbie kept on scanning the road ahead. Then he put down the binoculars. "Get off at the next exit," he said. "We've lost him."

43

The town of Milton was established in 1710, according to the welcome sign, and from the looks of that sign and the looks of the houses, it had kept a tight ass-hole ever since. It would be hard to build a community that looked more prim. It was all very neat and clean and historical and nauseating. Herbie directed me through it. He didn't seem discouraged, but I was discouraged as hell.

"What are we doing here?" I said.

"Playing the odds," Herbie said. "You have your money?" I nodded. "How much?"

"Thirty-six dollars."

"That should be enough," Herbie said, "if we can get enough change. We're going to have a problem."

"Change?"

"Dimes," Herbie said. He directed me to a large, modern drugstore. We walked to the back, past the counters of Nytol, E-Z Doz, Sleeptite, Awake!, Rouse, Bufferin, Anacin, Contac, and all the other pills. Behind the druggists' counter there were giant bottles of pills, the tranqs, bennies, and sleepers that you needed a prescription for. We went straight to the back, where there were three telephone booths, with the phone books hanging from a wall rack.

"Okay," Herbie said. "We assume, because we have to, that he's going home. And home is south of Boston, since he was on the Southeast Expressway. And probably within an hour of commuting. Okay. We know his last name is Murphy. What's his first name?"

I tried to remember. "Roger, I think. Anyway, something with R."

"Good. And his rank?"

"Lieutenant."

"Good," Herbie said, opening the directory. "Go get your change."

And then we began. We each took one column of Murphys. I took the left column, beginning with Murphy, Ralph A. Herbie took the right column, beginning with Murphy, Roland J. And we called. All of my calls were the same.

"Hello?"

"Hello," I would say, "is Lieutenant Murphy there?"

"Who?"

For the first few, I would mumble some excuse, or say wrong number. Later, I got so that when I heard "Who?" I just hung up. Alongside me, in the next booth, Herbie was doing the same thing. I heard the clink each time he put in another dime.

Finally, around the fifteenth time: "Hello?"

"Hello, is Lieutenant Murphy there?"

"Not at the moment."

I sighed and smiled. At last. "When do you expect him back?"

"Not until tomorrow night. He's on weekend maneuvers at Fort Devens. Who's calling please?"

"Sorry," I said, "wrong number."

At the bottom of my column were the Roger Murphys. I missed on Roger A., Roger J., Roger M., Roger N. Finally I got Roger V.

"Hello, is Lieutenant Murphy there?"

"No, but I expect him any minute. Who's calling?"

"Uh, this is Captain Fry."

"Captain Fry?" She obviously didn't know any Captain Fry.

"Yes. I'm down at the Fourth stationhouse now. I wanted to see your husband. I guess I just missed him."

"Yes," she said, "you must have. Can I have him call you back?"

"No, thanks," I said. "I'll call back later on."

"What did you say your name was again?" she asked.

"Nice to talk to you, Mrs. Murphy," I said, and hung up.

I had my finger on the line. Murphy, Roger V., 43 Crescent Lane, Ackley.

44

"How much left?" Herbie said, as we drove away from the drugstore.

"How much what?"

"Money," Herbie said.

I shrugged, and handed him all the dimes I had, and the few dollar bills the drugstore hadn't been able to change.

"You're in luck," Herbie said. "Fifteen dollars."

"Why am I in luck?"

"Make your next left, and the left after that."

I followed his directions, and came to the E-Z Car

Rental. Lowest Rates on Compacts and Other Fine Cars.

I parked. "What are we doing?"

"Getting a new car," Herbie said. "They'll take fifteen dollars here as a deposit."

We got out and went inside and talked to H. Lewis, Prop. It turned out he wouldn't take fifteen dollars as the deposit. He would take fifty dollars, and not a penny less.

"We don't have fifty dollars," Herbie said patiently.

"That's it, then," Mr. Lewis said, behind the counter.

"Come on," Herbie said. "Give us a break."

"Sorry."

"Come on. We'll leave the VW with you."

Mr. Lewis looked out the window at Herbie's VW. "Probably hot," he said.

"Come on," Herbie said. "Who'd steal a VW?" The man squinted at him. "Look," Herbie said, "I've got the registration for it and everything. It's not stolen. Give us a car for fifteen."

"No."

"Come on, Mister, we got dates tonight, and if we don't get there . . ."

"Use your VW."

"We can't. It's overheating. It'll blow out on us if we drive any farther."

The man sighed. We both tried to look as pitiable as possible. Finally he said, "Where're the girls from?"

"What girls?"

"Your dates."

"Oh. Currier College."

Mr. Lewis sighed. His face softened. He looked at me, then at Herbie, and he smiled.

"Currier College, eh?" His smile got broader.

"Yeah," we both smiled. "Currier College."

"Heh, heh, good old Currier," he said, beginning to chuckle and shake his head with memories.

"Yeah, right, good old Currier," we both said, chuckling.

He was laughing openly now. "No wonder you want a bigger car," he said. "Got to have a bigger car."

"Yeah, right, got to be bigger." He was laughing and shaking his head as he gave us the keys. "I remember how it was, I sure do," he said. Herbie started filling out the forms. "Just remember, boys, no stains on the back seat. I don't want to see any stains."

45

Forty-three Crescent Drive in Ackley was not in a rundown neighborhood, but it wasn't spiffy, either. The house was small. There was a faded, red, 1956 Ford sedan in the driveway, and Murphy's Narc Special, the green one, parked in the street out front.

Down the street some kids were playing stickball. The Murphy house was quiet. As the evening grew darker, a small boy of five or six came out and rode his bicycle around the house, down the drive, and into the street. As we watched, he joined the stickball game.

We were parked a couple of houses up, in what Herbie called our "inconspicuous" car, a canary-yellow Corvair with one front headlamp knocked out. It was all we had been able to get for fifteen dollars but at least, as he kept saying, it wasn't the VW.

About half an hour passed. It was now quite dark. Pretty soon Murphy came out, his jacket off, his tie loosened. In one hand he held his dinner napkin. He came out into the street and looked up and down, then whistled once, shrilly.

He waited, looking up and down. He whistled again.

And then his son came back, pedaling furiously, and I thought, That poor, scared kid, with an old man like that. And the kid streaked up the drive, jumped off his bike, and ran up to his father, who bent over and scooped him up, and hugged him while the kid beamed, and they both went inside.

"Well, he can't be all bad," Herbie said.

"Don't be a sucker," I said.

We waited another hour. I got to thinking about the writer who said you are what you pretend to be. I'd thought about that and decided it was wrong, that you became what you were least afraid of becoming; and that was a much more dangerous thing, because it was much more basic and much more subtle. You are what you are least afraid of becoming . . .

I'd had some good times with that theory. It had led me to believe that no one could even imagine what it was that he really wanted unless he first lost the fear of his own imagination. And he couldn't begin to do that without an opportunity. I mean, you can't expect the president of Dow Chemical to suddenly go out and join the peace marchers. He simply hasn't got time to think about such things. He's the president, for Christ's sake—all he wants to know is if the marches are hurting the sale of Saran Wrap. And in the same light, you can't expect Huey Newton to join the police force next chance he gets, because it's not exactly his trip.

So I devised a little scheme whereby everyone in the country, for one day out of each month, had to assume the role of the person or persons whose station and intellect he feared most. It was quite delightful, figuring out what everyone's role would be. J. Edgar Hoover spent the day stoned in a commune in Arizona. Spiro Agnew had to hawk copies of *Muhammed Speaks* in front of Grand Central Station. Radical student politicos took over the police departments of the nation. Lester Maddox shined shoes in Watts. Walter Hickel dropped acid in the Grand Canyon. Julius Hoffman served Panther breakfasts to school children in S.F. And Richard Nixon was allowed to do anything in the world that he wanted to do, so long as he did it right.

"Oh-oh," Herbie said.

I sat up straighter in the seat. It was quite dark now; the street and the neighborhood were completely silent. Murphy was coming out of his house. He had his jacket back on, but no briefcase. And no other baggage.

I frowned as I watched. "What does that mean?"

"I don't know," said Herbie.

Murphy got into the red car, backed out, and headed down the road, with us behind.

46

He went north and turned off at the Roxbury exit. That was a little bit of a surprise, but not much. Roxbury was as good a place as any.

While I drove, I said to Herbie, "You got the Baggies?"

"Yeah."

"And the piece?"

"Yeah. All set." Then he giggled.

"What's funny?"

"I'm nervous," Herbie said.

I was nervous, too. We could get really fucked up doing this cops-and-robbers riff.

Murphy turned onto Mass Avenue, still going north. He drove past the hospital, then turned right on Columbia.

"Maybe he's getting a little action," Herbie said, and giggled again.

"Will you cut that out?" I said.

"Sorry."

Murphy drove up Columbia. He went straight past the hookers without even slowing down.

Herbie said, "Slow down."

"Why?"

"I want to look."

"Shit, Herbie." I kept going, right after Murphy. He went up five blocks, and turned right again, onto a side street, where he parked. I parked and watched as he got out of his car, walked around to the back, opened the trunk, and removed a large suitcase.

"Far out," I said, to no one in particular.

Herbie started to get out of the car to follow Murphy, but I pushed him back. "My turn," I said. I got out and followed him down the street a short distance, then watched as he climbed the steps of one of the old brownstones. He kicked aside some broken glass, which clinked down the steps to the sidewalk. I paused a moment, then followed him up, my shoes making a crunching sound on the glass.

At the ground level, I paused once again. I could hear Murphy going up the steps. I opened the door and stepped into the hallway. Then, cautiously, I looked up the stairwell. I saw his hand grip the banister as he went up to the third floor. Then his hand disappeared, and he paused, and I saw him leaning back against the railing. A knock, then the door opened and he moved out of sight.

I waited there a moment, then took off back to the car.

"You find it?" Herbie said.

"Yeah. Third floor on the right."

"Good. How many?"

I was sitting down, fumbling for a cigarette with trembling fingers. "How many what?"

"Voices. Didn't you go up and listen at the door?"

"Are you crazy?"

"That's what I would have done," he said and, looking at him, I realized it was true.

"You are crazy."

"It's important to know how many people are in that room," he said.

"We'll find out soon enough."

"That's true," Herbie said. "Only it would be nice to know before we find out."

"Yeah, well."

Silence. I smoked and tried to get my hands under control. In the back of my head was the feeling that this might work after all, that we might really pull it off. I hadn't really believed that all day. I didn't expect we'd get this far, and in some ways I had hoped we wouldn't get this far. Because from now on the trip was for real.

Murphy came out of the brownstone about ten minutes later. He was empty-handed, and he whistled "As the Caissons Go Rolling Along" as he got into his car.

We waited a few minutes after he'd driven off, and then Herbie said, "Ready?"

I nodded.

We got out of the car and walked to the brownstone.

47

It is wrong to say we were nervous. We were terrified. We stood in the ground-floor hallway of the brownstone, smelling the combination of old cabbage, urine, dust, and mildew which hung in the air. As we started up the stairs, Herbie gave me the gun. "Just remember," he said. "Watch your fingers."

"Is it loaded?" I asked. It felt light for a piece.

"Yeah," said Herbie. "Just watch your fingers. If they see——"

"Okay, okay."

We came to the third-floor landing and walked around to the door. Herbie moved forward and I stayed behind him, keeping the gun out of sight, as we had agreed. Staring at the door, I had a vision of a six-foot-six, two-hundred-forty-pound spade standing behind it, just waiting to grind up a couple of college punks.

Herbie knocked, looked back at me, and smiled. Herbie was enjoying himself, in his own nervous little way. He didn't know any better, I thought.

He knocked and waited. Nothing happened. Right at that point I was ready to forget the whole thing and leave, but Herbie knocked again, louder. Then I heard soft footsteps inside. They didn't sound like the footsteps of anybody big; I began to feel better.

A voice said, "Who is it?" Herbie glanced back at me, uncertain what to say. "Who's there?" said the voice.

"Murphy," I growled. As soon as I said it, I knew it was stupid. Murphy wouldn't use his real name with a Roxbury front.

Behind the door, a pause. "Who?"

There was nothing to do but barge ahead. "Murphy," I said, in a louder voice. "I'm twenty bucks short."

We heard the chain rattling. Then the door opened and a pimply, white creature nosed into view and said, "Listen, you counted it right in front——"

He broke off, staring at us. He started to slam the door, but Herbie got his foot in. "One moment," Herbie said. "We wish to make you a business proposition."

I pushed Herbie from behind and there was a creaking and then the soft crunch of rotten wood breaking as the chain lock ripped out of the door. We stepped into the room and the cat jumped back and stared at us.

"B-business," he said, "I-I'ma not innarested."

The last word came out in a tumble and as I looked at him I saw why. He was thin and pale and his pupils were tiny. Arms covered with tracks. Speed freak. Probably paranoid as hell to begin with, I thought, without a couple of dudes barging into his room and pulling a piece on him. Then I realized that the way we were standing, he wouldn't be able to see the piece, and I moved aside from Herbie enough so that he could dig it. He crumpled on the floor and babbled as Herbie said, "Hear us out. We have no intention of doing you any bodily harm." He paused to look around the room. "You seem quite capable of taking care of that yourself." At this the guy only babbled some more, the words flowing out in an unintelligible staccato, and groveled on the floor. "Please sit down," Herbie said, giggling again, and the guy pulled himself over to the single mattress in the room and collapsed. The room was definitely a speed freak's home-sweet-home. The walls were peeling and there was the one mattress and a couple of posters that covered the places that were peeling the worst. The floor was littered with empty soda cans and candy wrappers, and right next to the mattress was a set of works and an old spoon in a glass of water. Ho hum. A couple of bags of what looked like hydrochloride. Nothing else.

By this time the cat was speaking in sentences.

"Listen," he said, "I don't got no money, honest I don't——"

Herbie motioned him to be silent. "We don't want your money," he said. "We have an offer to make."

The guy jumped up, and I waved the gun at him. "Don't mess with me," I said, doing my best to sound lethal. "I'm getting nervous with this piece." He sat down again and Herbie went over and started fooling with the telephone. It was my rap.

"Okay," I said, "here's the deal. We're willing to give you two hundred and fifty, a good fucking price, for every one of those bricks Murphy laid on you."

"Bu-but," he said, and I looked down at the piece.

"Murphy," I said, "the cat who was just in here. We'll give you two-fifty for every one of his bricks. Think about it. You could be out of town before they even knew you'd gone wrong on them. And you wouldn't have to shoot that shit any more . . ." waving the gun in the direction of the hydrochloride. "Get it? You'd be a rich man. Nothing but pure meth, pure coke, anything you wanted. Pure. No more street shit for you, brother."

He looked at me, or rather squinted, with new respect. I had touched his frame of reference. The word *meth,* the very idea of pure meth, filled his mind and a soft glow spread over his face. An involuntary "Wow!" seeped out of him.

"Okay," I said, "now you got the picture. And all you

gotta do for that bread is produce those bricks." The words broke his reverie.

"Lissen, fe-fe-fellas, I'd like to he-help ya, ba-but I can't tell you what I don't know, da-dig? I don't have a-nothing. Da-dig? I'm a dra-drop, dra-drop, I'm a drop-off man. They give me the ra-room and I pay out the bread. I never seen a bra-brick for two years now, da-dig? The cats come in here and I pa-pay 'em what I got." He stopped and looked at the piece. "Honest."

"Listen, Speedy," I said, "we haven't got the time, da-dig?" Herbie laughed. "Now who pays for this room and who gets the stuff and who sets you up with guys like Murphy?"

"Mm Ma-Murphy?" he said, or rather tried to say.

"The punk who was just in here, the pig you paid off. Who sets you up with him?"

"Th-th-that guy's a pa-pig?" said Speedy, incredulous.

"Herbie," I said, "he's gonna need a little work." Herbie nodded. He was enjoying the whole thing tremendously.

"You got the silencer, just in case?" he said, and I smiled grimly.

"Na-No! Fellas, ha, ha, honest!" He sounded like he had hay fever. "I'll tell yah what I know. A sp-spade dude I met on the street seh-seh-sets me up, honest. Tha-that's all."

"Herbie," I said, cold as ice. "Check the mattress." Herbie went over to the mattress as I motioned Speedy off with a wave of the piece.

"Hey," he said, "ha-who do you think you are?"

"Unless you wanna find out, you better shut up," I said. Herbie lifted the mattress and there, lo and behold, were our bricks. "Pull 'em out!" I said to Herbie.

"Ha-hey!" said Speedy, suddenly realizing what was going on. "You ca-can't take those. The ma-man's coming by tonight for th-those!"

"Well, then, we'd better be on our way," I said. "Herbie, put the stuff in the sack and let's leave this punk to his works." Spoken in the best tough-guy, out-of-the-corner-of-the-mouth tones I could muster. Speedy was not impressed.

"Ha-hey! What about my br-bread?"

"Shut up, punk," I said, but just as Herbie turned his back on him the freak lunged for the bag of bricks, and they were both down on the floor.

"Up," I shouted. "Get up unless you wanna eat some lead," and he stood up, leaving Herbie rolling around on the floor, laughing.

"Too much," Herbie said. "Eat some lead. Too much."

Speedy looked at Herbie, then back at me, and stepped forward with a lead-be-damned gleam in his eyes. "Pa-punk, heh?" he gurgled. "Punk, punk, alla ta-time punk, heh? Whozza pa-pa-unk?"

He was only about a yard away from me and I was thinking we had to get out of there fast. "Stay back," I said. "Back!"

But he kept on coming and finally I felt myself getting excited and desperate at the same time, and a strange feeling was welling up inside of me, power, a power feeling, his fate in my hands, and all of a sudden I knew that his fate was in my hands, and I felt the rush of it, I'm going to do it I rushed, I'm going to do it, and I pulled the trigger thinking simultaneously

O my God I've done it O my God what have I done I've done it——

And just then a fine stream of water arced out of the gun, hitting Speedy in the knees.

He was so freaked he didn't understand for a minute, but then he knew what had happened and jumped at me. Herbie was on the floor again laughing, and I knew that I was going to have to put Speedy away for a while to get us out of there in one piece. Fortunately speed freaks are not noted for their muscle tone. A quick right to the temple brought him to the floor and then I dropped down on him, knee first, and caught him in the crotch. Another right and a left to the jaw and he was gone. It'd look better that way, I thought, when the man showed up. I pulled Herbie up from the floor and we ran.

We were almost to the door when the first gunshot echoed through the hallway, and the banister nearby splintered. We dropped to the ground, ducking back into the shadows.

"Oh shit, oh shit, oh shit," Herbie said. He was too scared to say anything else.

I looked up toward the third floor. A cloud of pale blue smoke hung in the air. I started to move downward again, and there was another gunshot. This time I saw the flame spurt from the rifle. Speedy was up there, all right. But his shot was wide—he couldn't hit anything in his condition.

"Come on," I said, "he can't hit anything."

"The hell he can't," Herbie said, crouched down behind the splintered banister.

All around us, the apartment building was beginning to wake up. We heard people moving and talking in their rooms. No doors opened, though; everybody was afraid to look outside. On the other hand, they'd certainly be phoning the heat.

"Come on, Herbie!"

For a moment he stayed curled up, paralyzed, and then he sprang forward. We sprinted downstairs. There were two more shots. And then, just as we were going out the door, a final shot and Herbie shouted, "I'm hit, I'm hit!" He stumbled and fell through the front door and lay on the steps.

I was already halfway down the steps when I heard him cry out. I ran back up, knowing that Speedy would now be racing from the stairwell to the outside window. I grabbed the bag that Herbie had dropped, and helped him to his feet. He was wincing with pain.

"Got me . . . in the shoulder . . . bad . . ." Herbie said. I put my arm around his waist and got him down the steps and off to the car. There was one more shot as we drove off into the night.

48

The nearest place was Sandra's apartment. It took us about ten minutes to get there, ten very bad minutes, with Herbie trying to be manful about things but not succeeding very well. He kept talking about how he could feel the blood running down his back. I wanted to take him to a doctor but he said No, no doctors, No —and anyway we couldn't go to a doctor with a carful of dope, so I drove to Sandra's. I got him up the steps to the apartment. John wasn't there; no one answered the buzzer. I reached up above the door, found the key, and unlocked the door.

John and Sandra wouldn't dig Herbie's blood all over the apartment, but that was just too bad for now. I threw the sack of dope inside, then helped Herbie down the hallway to the bedroom. He was groaning softly, and covered with sweat.

"Easy now, easy," I said, helping him down onto the bed. "Let's get your jacket off." He moaned as I removed it, his face contorted; with the jacket off, I got him onto his stomach and pulled out his shirt, which I then tore straight up the back to see how bad the wound was.

And stopped.

For a flash I was puzzled, and then I began to get pissed. Fucking Herbie. "Where does it hurt, man?"

"Oh . . . oh . . . in the middle . . . right shoulder . . . around the scap . . . scapula."

"Yes," I said. "I see." What I saw was a smooth, slightly flabby, white expanse of unbroken skin. "Doesn't look too bad, though. Here, you better see for yourself. Go look in the mirror."

"Okay," Herbie said, doing the heavy number. With a wince he said, "Give me a hand up, Pete, buddy."

"Sure." I whipped him off the bed with one hand and watched in silence as he staggered to his feet and walked into the bathroom. The bathroom light went on, and there was a long silence.

Finally, quietly, came an awed voice: "Far out."

There then followed another long silence, in which I lit a cigarette, smoked it, and tried to keep from going in and plugging the little bastard myself. After a while, I heard him say, "Most perplexing." And then, finally, he came back into the bedroom.

"I know what you're thinking," Herbie said. He was being very dignified and composed. "And I apologize for being an alarmist." And then he walked out of the room.

"Hey, where're you going?" I went out into the hallway after him, and found him returning with the sack. He walked toward the kitchen, and as he passed me, he said, "I think we'd better count the bricks, don't you?"

He had made a fast recovery, and I told him so. He didn't say anything in response. Out in the kitchen, he began to count the bricks while I raided Sandra's refrigerator. Sandra is a candy freak. Every kind of American, Italian, French, Spanish, Swiss, Indonesian, Japanese candy can be found in her refrigerator. While I was looking, I said, "How many bricks?"

"What?" Preoccupied voice.

"How many bricks?"

"C'mere and dig this, Peter."

I turned around to look. He was holding the sack in front of him. At first I saw nothing. Then, to demonstrate, he stuck his finger into the neat little hole.

"Interesting?" he said. He then picked up one of the bricks, and cut it open with a knife before I could protest. There was a piece of dull gray metal imbedded in the brick.

I went over and plucked it out. "Far out," I said.

"The bag was over my right shoulder," Herbie said.

"Far out," I said again.

"I believe you owe me an apology," Herbie said.

And then I began to laugh. "I owe you more than that," I said. "I owe you the biggest smoke of your life." I got a piece of newspaper and tore off a quarter, and pulled off a chunk of brick and began to roll it into a joint.

As Herbie watched, he said with a small smile, "All in all, it was pretty exciting, wasn't it?"

§

An hour later, we were still in the kitchen, drafting the statement. We were both very stoned and very happy. I was writing and Herbie was dictating. I said, "How about 'Please release her tomorrow morning'?"

"No," Herbie said. "Make it strong. 'I want her released tomorrow morning'—and then put in the D.A. and the *Globe* and all that."

I nodded, and made the changes.

"Is that it?" Herbie said.

"That's it," I said, and picked up the phone to call. The first three times I dialed, I got the siren whine of a nonexistent number. Finally, the fourth time, it began to ring. I was very, very stoned.

A woman's voice: "Hello?"

I said, "Lieutenant Murphy, please. This is Captain Fry of the Narcotics Division."

"Just a minute, Captain."

A long silence at the other end of the phone, presumably while Murphy tried to figure out who the hell

Captain Fry was—or who would be calling saying he was Captain Fry. Or what Captain Fry would want at this time of night, if indeed there really were a Captain Fry, whom he had never heard of . . . God, I was zonked.

Finally: "Murphy here."

I jumped at the sound of his voice, the familiarity of it. For a moment I flashed back to Alameda County and the interrogation room, the kneeing, the whole riff. Then I got hold of myself. "Yes," I said. "This is a mutual acquaintance. I thought you would appreciate knowing that I have acquired twelve kilograms of marijuana that have an interesting set of fingerprints on them."

"Who is this?"

"The kilograms are stamped with a peace symbol and the numbers eight nine oh, which allows their California origin to be quite reliably established. The fingerprints," I continued, "are yours and Susan Blake's. That is an interesting combination. It is easy to explain how that combination of fingerprints got there. But I wonder, is it possible to explain how they came into my hands?"

"Who's calling?" Murphy said, his voice tense.

"I think that a lot of people would be curious enough to be interested in my explanation," I said. "I have one very curious acquaintance in the district attorney's office, and another at the *Boston Globe*."

There was a long, taut silence. Murphy was thinking it over. And he was going to play it our way, I knew. He had no choice. He'd have to drop charges on Sukie.

"What do you want?" he said, finally.

"I want the girl released and all charges dropped."

There was a long, slow sigh at the other end. The bastard obviously wasn't used to having other people play as rough as he did. Finally he cleared his throat.

"Now you listen to me, punk, and listen good. You can't touch me, you can't even rile me. You go near the D.A.'s office with those bricks and I'll see to it personally that you get busted. Now. As far as I'm concerned, you can go right ahead and do anything you want. I'm going back to bed." *Click!*

Herbie had been sitting across the table from me. He must have seen my face fall. "What happened?" he said.

I couldn't believe it. I was shaking my head, absolutely not believing it. "He didn't go for it," I said.

49

I was suddenly ghastly sober, the kind of sober where the room lights seem brighter and the shadows sharper and everything is a little bit uglier. I got up and poured myself a Scotch—some of John's Chivas this time, the hell with him. I felt it slosh down in my stomach over the Perugina chocolate, and I thought about Speedy shooting at us, and I began to feel sick. I spent a few hours standing there, leaning against the wall, trying to decide whether I would make it or not, and finally decided I wouldn't. I jumped for the sink.

"Flawless," Herbie said.

I turned and looked back at him. The world was green. "Thanks," I said.

"I meant the plan," Herbie said, ignoring me as I wiped my mouth with a towel. He ticked the points off on his fingers. "Murphy is fronting bricks. His prints are on them. We recover the fronted bricks. We threaten to expose him unless he releases the girl. He releases the girl. We expose him anyway. A flawless plan."

"It didn't work," I said again. "You can't bust pigs, no matter how fucked-up they are."

Herbie nodded in a puzzled way. "He must have protection," he said. "That's the only answer."

I laughed, and as I did the green world shifted back to glaring white. "Uh-uh," I said. "He doesn't give a crap, that's all. He knows that a couple of punk kids are trying to rip him off, and he doesn't mind a bit. He knows they can't touch him. The day when freaks bust wrong pigs is the day that——"

"I find that difficult to believe," Herbie said, sounding for all the world like my old man.

"Yeah, well, that's what's happening." I was beginning to see what it meant, from Murphy's viewpoint, to be hassled by a couple of kids. And I began to see just how little power we had. Nobody ever had power unless someone gave it to them. Murphy wasn't giving us an inch.

"Maybe he doesn't think we can do it," Herbie said.

"Maybe we can't," I said. It had all been an enormous bluff. We didn't know anybody on the newspapers, or at the D.A.'s office. We didn't know anybody, period.

John chose that happy moment to walk in with Sandra. She ran for the john, and he came into the kitchen, sniffing the air. "Jesus, it stinks in here." He walked over to the sink, took a look, and shook his head. "Harkness, you never could——"

"And you couldn't either," I said. "Get bent, or get lost, or preferably both."

John paused to savor the atmosphere. "What've you dudes been up to?"

"The impossible," Herbie said.

Then John saw the bricks on the kitchen table. His spirits rose. "My, my, what have we here?"

Nobody said anything.

"Fine stuff," he said, crumbling a bit between his fingers. "Almost as good as——" He stopped, looked at another brick, at the stamp on the wrapper. "Where'd you pick this up?"

He looked over at me. I didn't say anything. So he looked over at Herbie. "Three guesses," Herbie said. John just stood there, totally out of it, and then Sandra walked in and began clucking about the smell. I was feeling a little sick again. John saw the bottle of Chivas out and began bitching about my drinking his stuff again. All I could think of was how we couldn't touch Murphy. It didn't seem possible that he was untouchable. It wasn't possible. It couldn't be possible.

"Herbie," I said, "we can do it."

"How's that?" Herbie sounded bored.

"We could arrange a trade."

"No!" He sat suddenly upright. "That ruins everything. The whole point of the plan——"

"I know," I said. "But the flawless plan didn't work.

We already know that. The only thing we can do is trade."

"You mean," Herbie said, his mouth turning down in distaste, "*give* him the bricks?"

"Give who the bricks?" John said sharply. He had suddenly forgotten all about the Scotch.

"Yes," I said. "Give them to him."

"That's nowhere," Herbie said. "That's greasing the wheels, playing right into the system. Greasing Murphy's wheels."

"What's going on?" John demanded. He seemed almost frightened by not knowing what was going on. A power trip that he wasn't part of. Frightening.

"We'd be playing right into it anyway," I said, "if we tried to buy her off on Monday."

"It's not the same," Herbie said. "You got to believe in justice sometime. You got to believe that if this stuff went to the papers, and the district attorney——"

"No," I said. I didn't believe it. And for some reason, I remembered a conversation I'd once had with my father about Boston justice. I was telling him how Super Spade got busted, and then bought himself off. He refused to believe the story. I tried to make him believe it—believe that everyone in Boston, from the mayor to the garbage collectors, was crooked. "But think what that means, or would mean if it were true," my father said. I had never thought about it. Not really. But I was thinking now.

"It won't work," Herbie said. "Even if he agrees, he'll take the bricks and keep the chick anyway."

"Maybe not," I said.

"Maybe not," Herbie mimicked. "You going to trust him?"

"Will somebody please tell me what the hell is going on here?" John shouted.

But by that time I was checking through Sandra's silverware, plucking at the tines of her forks, trying to find one that sounded good. And when I finally did, I picked up the phone and dialed.

"You're crazy," Herbie said.

"Who're you calling?" John said. His voice had a slight whine now, a very atypical voice for John. I began to see him differently.

This time, a male voice answered the phone directly. An irritable male: "Hello."

"Lieutenant Murphy?" I said. I looked over at Herbie and John. John was beginning to get the picture. His mouth was open.

"Yeah."

"Is this Lieutenant Murphy?" I said again.

"Yeah."

"I'm calling with a business proposition and——"

"Not interested. Goodbye——"

"Wait," I said. I had a flash of desperation. But the bastard waited. I could hear him breathing at the other end. "I've got twelve bricks here," I said. "They were . . . borrowed from a gentleman in Boston. As you know, their market value is in the neighborhood of three thousand dollars. I'd like you to have them."

"What for?" He was growling, but he was interested.

"All we want is the girl," I said. "Drop charges and release her. We'll get the twelve bricks to you."

"That's not good enough, sonny," Murphy said. "Goodbye."

By now, though, I knew he wasn't going to hang up. "As a demonstration of faith," I said, "we will arrange for you to receive four bricks tonight. You'll get the rest on her release."

"Six bricks," Murphy said.

"Six bricks?" I said. "That seems an awful lot."

"Six bricks," Murphy said, "and not one less."

"You're not being very reasonable, Lieutenant Murphy," I said. "But if you want six bricks, then . . ." and here I plucked the tines of the fork ". . . six it will be."

"What was that?" Murphy said.

"Are we agreed on six bricks?" I said. And I plucked the tines once more. It didn't make a very realistic sound, but then, it didn't have to.

"What was that noise?"

"We'll call you in an hour," I said, "to tell you where you can collect the bricks. Is that satisfactory?"

"What was that noise?" But he knew damned well what the noise was, or thought he knew.

"We want you to be honest," I said. "That's just our way of keeping things up front. We'll talk to you in an hour." And I hung up.

Herbie was staring at me. "Far out," he said.

John said, "What was the fork stuff?"

"Brilliant," Herbie said, "brilliant. We can drop the bricks at the Museum of Science, and——"

"What was the fork?" John said.

I plucked it again, and listened to the brief *twink* it made. "Our tape recorder," I said, and began to laugh.

50

"Murphy's forked himself," Herbie laughed. I was laughing so hard there were tears in my eyes.

Only John wasn't laughing. He was frowning and staring at the bricks. Then he frowned and stared at us. And finally he said, "He'll still rip you off."

"Who?" I said. "Murphy? After we taped him?"

"Yeah," John said. He didn't explain. He just sat back and watched us as we stopped laughing slowly, the laughs turning into coughs, and then silence.

"What do you mean?" Herbie said.

"I mean," John said, "that Murphy is going to sit back and ask himself what kind of taping device makes a beeping noise. And he's going to decide that only a commercial device does—like they use for telephone interviews on the news radios and stuff. And he's going to decide that a bunch of snot-nosed kids don't have a commercial device, that they have a kitchen fork and are trying to rip him off."

I shook my head. "He's not that smart."

I looked over at Herbie for confirmation. Herbie was staring at his feet.

John said, "Murphy'll take your six bricks, keep the girl, and figure out a way to bust you later on."

"No way," I said, and laughed. But John wasn't laughing, and Herbie wasn't laughing. And I began thinking about Murphy, and the interrogation room in San Francisco, and I began to think that maybe they were right on. Murphy was a pig—the pig.

I stood up. "All right," I said. "The only way is to arrange a trade."

John shook his head. "Who do you think you're messing with, man?"

But by now I was thinking very fast, and seeing things clearly. Seeing how it could be done. I picked up the phone again.

"What're you doing?" Herbie said.

I just dialed the number.

§

There is no building in Boston quite like South Station. It'll be torn down soon for some new structure, but in the meantime, it is unique: giant, cavernous, dirty, and deserted. Especially at three o'clock in the morning. The faint smell of piss hung over everything—the dirty walls, the cracked wooden benches, the handful of sailors and derelicts who were sitting around.

I arrived by taxi and walked in the west entrance. It had once been pretty fashionable, with a broad metal overhead canopy leading through six swinging doors to the inside. Just back of the doors were rows of telephone booths. I paused at one to take down the number. Then I went back outside. There was a taxi rank lined up at the curb, the drivers sitting back in their cars, smoking cigarettes. I went to the first cab and said to the driver, "I want you to do me a favor."

"Sure," he said. "You and the President."

I held out a ten-spot. He looked appeased. "What's the story?"

"In half an hour," I said, "a man will get into your taxi and say he is a police officer. Ask to see his identification. If he produces it, drive him to the Newton tolls. This should cover everything." I wagged the ten dollar bill.

"That right?" the driver said.

"This is police business," I said gravely.

"It don't sound——"

"Okay," I said, and started down the line toward the second taxi.

"Just a minute!"

I went back and looked at my driver. His name, I could read on the seat-plate identification card, was Joseph V. Murphy. Naturally.

"Just a minute," he said. "The Newton tolls?"

"Yeah."

"Fifteen bucks and I'll take him. That covers my waiting time. I might get a customer, you know."

I looked around the deserted station entrance. What the hell. "Okay," I said. "Fifteen." I gave him the money, and made a production out of writing down his name and license number. He watched me do it.

"What's this all about?" he said.

"Undercover," I said. "Narcotics division." The cabby looked at me. Then he looked at the fifteen dollars. Then he nodded, and I went back inside.

The first part was completed. I re-checked the telephone number in the booth. I sat in the booth and looked out. From where I sat, I could see through to the street and to the warehouses beyond. There were dozens of windows, all dark, in the buildings across the street.

Perfect.

Whistling now, I went into the innards of the station. A train was pulling up on one of the far tracks; I heard the metallic screech of brakes and the hiss of steam. Otherwise, it was silent. A half-dozen sailors sat laughing drunkenly on one of the benches near the center of the room. I went over and sat down next to them, placing my nondescript suitcase (an old one of Sandra's, wiped of prints) at my feet. The sailors ignored me. After a moment I leaned over toward the nearest one and said, "I got to take a leak. Watch my bag?"

"Yeah, sure," the sailor said, and kept on talking with his friends. I wandered off.

Fifteen minutes to go. I kept glancing at my watch. I looked back at the sailors, wondering if they'd decide to take off with the bag or maybe open it. But they weren't paying any attention. I went over to the train schedules, pretended to read them, and then wandered over to a far corner of the station, where there were more telephone booths. I sat down in one of them. I could barely see the booths near the entrance; they were perhaps a hundred yards away, and down a slight incline.

I waited.

I kept thinking of things that could go wrong. A million things could go wrong. For instance, he could flood the place with narcs—but that would mean he'd have to split the take, or else he'd have to play it straight. Too much bread in it for that to happen. Unless Murphy was going to be honest. A dreary thought.

I waited some more.

At three-thirty I looked over at the west entrance. Nobody there. Five more minutes passed, and still no one arrived. I was beginning to worry. And then I saw him come through the doors.

Sukie was with him. No cuffs. He'd done it—he'd gotten her off, charges dropped, and brought her to South Station for the exchange. Just as I'd told him.

For a moment, I felt exhilaration, and then caution. Murphy stood with Sukie in the center of the west entrance, waiting. He said something to her; she shook her head.

I put my dime into the receiver and dialed. Faintly, I could hear the phone ringing in the booth near where she was standing with Murphy. They ignored it for a moment. Then Murphy looked over at the pay phone. One pay phone in a row of twelve just doesn't start ringing at three-thirty in the morning for no reason. He went over to answer it.

"Hello?"

"Good morning, lieutenant."

I could see his body stiffen. He started looking around, back toward the inside of the station, and then outside.

"Forget that," I said. "I'm where I can see you, and you can't see me—unless you want to search a lot of buildings." That one worked; he was looking out toward the warehouses.

"Is the girl free?"

"Yeah."

"Let me talk to her a minute."

"I want those——"

"Let me talk to her. I'm watching you."

"You son of a ——"

"You want to blow it, Murphy? And have to book her again? What would they think about that, down at the station?"

There was a long silence. Then he waved Sukie over. He remained sitting in the booth. He held his hand over the receiver, said something to her, and then gave her the phone.

"Hello?"

"Sukie," I said, "don't speak. Just listen. I want you to answer yes or no to my questions. Have you been released?"

"Yes."

"Have charges been dropped?"

"Yes."

"Is Murphy alone?"

"I think so."

"All right. Give the phone back to him."

She did. I watched Murphy take the receiver. "All right now you little——"

"First of all," I said, "send the girl to stand by the information booth in the center of the station. Then go over to the sailors inside. You'll see a black suitcase near one of them. The suitcase contains six bricks. Go check that."

"What about the rest?"

"I'll tell you about it."

Murphy put down the receiver. He said something to Sukie, who walked away from him. Then he went over to the sailors and demanded the suitcase. They protested. He flashed his badge. They gave it to him. He walked back to the telephone, sat down, opened the suitcase and checked.

"The bricks there?" I said.

"Yeah."

"All right. Here's how you get the rest. Go out to the taxi rank and get into the first cab. Say you are a policeman and show identification. The driver will take you to where the rest of the bricks are—and they'll be there, if nothing happens to the girl in the meantime. Understand?"

"Yeah." Very low.

"Anything happens to the girl between now and then, and by the time you get to the drop-off, the stuff'll be gone. Understand?"

"Yeah."

"Okay." And I hung up.

Murphy closed the suitcase and walked out toward the door. At the door he was met by three other men in raincoats. So he had been planning something, after all. He spoke to the men; they glanced at Sukie, standing alone in the middle of the station. The men went away. Murphy got into the cab.

The cab drove off.

It was over. I got out of the booth and went to the center of South Station, put my arms around her, and kissed her.

51

Murphy's trip to the Newton tolls was a waste of time. There was no more dope at the Newton tolls that night than there was on any other night. Six bricks wasn't much of a burn, but it was the best we could do for such a close friend.

All Sukie had to say in the taxi back to Cambridge was "How can those bastards arrest you and then decide, two days later, that they don't have enough evidence to hold you?"

"It's not easy," I said, laughing.

She laughed with me.

A Note on the Type

The text of this book was set in a type face called Primer, designed by Rudolph Ruzicka for the Mergenthaler Linotype Company and first made available in 1949. Primer, a modified modern face based on Century broadface, has the virtue of great legibility and was designed especially for today's methods of composition and printing.

Primer is Ruzicka's third typeface. In 1940 he designed Fairfield, and in 1947 Fairfield Medium, both for the Mergenthaler Linotype Company.

Ruzicka was born in Bohemia in 1883 and came to the United States at the age of eleven. He attended public schools in Chicago and later the Chicago Art Institute. During his long career he has been a wood engraver, etcher, cartographer, and book designer. For many years he was associated with Daniel Berkeley Updike and produced the annual keepsakes for The Merrymount Press from 1911 until 1941.

Ruzicka has been honored by many distinguished organizations, and in 1936 he was awarded the gold medal of the American Institute of Graphic Arts. From his home in New Hampshire, Ruzicka continues to be active in the graphic arts.

This book was composed,
printed and bound by The Book Press,
Brattleboro, Vermont.